Night Mission To Mogadishu

Trent LaLand

Hayden Publishing

Book edited by Jessica Gibson
Graphic Design: Kurt Metz
Book Cover Design: Donna Osborn Clark of Creation by Donna
Photocopy Images: Jackie Watters
Publishing Formatting & Branding web-designs: Ton'e Brown

Contact Information:
Hayden Publishing 2400 Old Milton Parkway, Suite #202
Alpharetta, Georgia 30009
678-439-8662
www.Haydenpublishinginc.com

Special Thanks to my reading fans and the support team who is a constant encouragement to my writings, you are loved deeply in my heart.

May God Bless and Enrich your life.
Trent LaLand

In memory of my wonderful parents Hilda and Rudolph LaLand and my sister Staff Sgt. Dalphia LaLand Johnson – US Marines

* * * * *

CONTENT

Foreword

As the author of this book, I never would have been a member of the Rescue Force that was diverted from Operation Desert Shield to the US Embassy in East Africa on a drastic rescue mission, if it had not been for my friend Scott Rush whom I ran on the track team with in high school, who persuaded me to join the Marines.

The mission received little notice and no media or press coverage, due to the fact that the upcoming war with Iraq demanded the media attention. Otherwise, the execution of such a short notice and high-risk operation might have garnered front-page headlines around the world.

I wanted to do a more extensive research for myself on what went wrong in Somali, Mogadishu. How the mission came about on such a short notice, and who was involved in the planning and phases of the mission.

I am writing this book to give recognition to the American and Foreign Nationals who were trapped in the middle of a horrifying civil war in war-torn East Africa in January 1991; US Ambassador to Somali, James K. Bishop, who went above and beyond using his great leadership and experience to protect and save not just the Americans, but also Foreign Nationals as well, and to his staff, security personnel, and the five Marine security guards who stood by his side during the crisis; to those who planned and set in motion Operation Eastern Exit, the US Navy and Marine Officers who planned the mission on board the Amphibious

Assault Ship U.S.S Guam LPH 9, the Air Force, Sailors and Marines who participated; and the Rescue Force who conducted the mission on the ground, which included myself.

It is a story about a mission that proves that Naval Expeditionary Forces can respond to any crisis in the world on a short notice, even when committed to larger Operations such as Operation Desert Shield. The mission proved to be dramatic as well as proficient. The mission itself seemed more like a Hollywood script rather than reality.

Trapped in the middle of a bloody civil war in Mogadishu, Somali, American Nationals, Foreign Diplomats and civilians had become the victims of gunfire and random acts of violence by armed looters, African Rebel Forces and Somali government forces, who have no regard for civilians or Diplomatic Privilege. There was no communication to the Mogadishu Airport, because the telephone lines to the airport had been cut. The US Ambassador James K. Bishop realized that the chances of escaping from Mogadishu's bloody civil war were becoming slim.

On 2 January 1991, he made a frantic call to Washington D.C. for rescue, briefing the State Department on the conditions on the ground in Mogadishu. His message was clear and frank stating that if a US Rescue Force did not arrive soon, there would be no one to rescue. His urgent call for help received immediate attention in Washington.

Acknowledgements

First and foremost, I would like to thank God for giving me the ability to bring this book to completion. Without Him, I would not have been able to possibly do this. Next, I would like to express my sincere thanks to my friends, church members and family members who gave up much of their time to assist me while I was writing this book. They were cooperative and generous with their involvement. There are too many to name, but they know who they are, and I want them to know how much they are appreciated.

Secondly, I would like to thank my editor Jessica Gibson and my publisher Ton'e Brown of Hayden Publishing Inc© for their continuous efforts and expert guidance in helping me to transform the thoughts in my head to something resembling reality. Without their abundant talent and patience, this book would not have been possible, and I feel very lucky to have them both as my editor, publisher as well as my friend.

Last but not least, I am deeply indebted to Kimberly Tillman and Andre Ballard for accommodating me with more time than I could have afforded, for sharing their knowledge and for numerous tips all of which culminated in the completion of this book; to Jackie Watters for taking time out of her hectic schedule to diligently help me by using her incredible God-given talent of insertion and the layout of pictures; and finally thank you to my brother Kevin LaLand who inspired me to write an account of the events that took place at the US Embassy in Mogadishu during January of 1991. I could not have brought this story

to fruition without their dedication in helping me bring this
book together.

Chapter 1

Before Boot Camp

1982 Indianapolis, Indiana, Arsenal Technical High School. It was my senior year. Like any other senior, I was making a decision concerning what my plans would be after high school. You go to college, land a job, sit around and do nothing, or join the military. By the second semester, most seniors have already decided what they are going to do. However, I was still undecided. Music was my minor, so I thought that would be the direction to go. I was on the track team and ran the 400 and the 4x400 relay. I ran third leg on the relay, and our anchorman Scott Rush was a horse.

Scott and I were stretching out at the City Track & Field Meet before the 4x400 relay when Rush told me that he signed up for the Marines. He stated, *"I'm shipping out for Boot Camp in September; you should sign up for the Marines too"*. I said I didn't know and that I would give it some thought, because I heard that the Marines was the toughest branch of the US Armed Forces. With me being a laid-back shy person, I felt that the Marines would not be a good fit for me. Graduation came fast after that conversation. On June 5, 1982 at Hinkle Field House Indianapolis, Indiana, we graduated from high school. Scott shipped out for Boot Camp that September just as he said he would.

I wasn't doing anything but playing basketball and going to the night clubs on the weekends. Scott graduated from Boot Camp in December 1982 and came home on leave for ten days, and we hooked up. He had his uniform on. I said to my self *"that Marine uniform looks good"*. Eventually I went downtown to the Marine recruiters' office with Scott, and he introduced me to recruiter Staff Sergeant Thomas Lee. The three of us went downtown to lunch. Scott talked about what Boot Camp was like, the training, and the Drill Instructors. After lunch we went back to Staff Sergeant Lee's office. Scott was working under Staff Sergeant Lee as a recruiter assistant for the ten days that he would be home on leave. He would accompany Staff Sergeant Lee to high schools and home visits of potential recruits. While at the office, Staff Sergeant Lee had me watch videos of Marine Corp Boot Camp Training, and Marine Duty Stations, Stateside and Overseas. I found myself going to the recruiter's office everyday talking to Staff Sergeant Lee and Scott. They were working hard trying to convince me to sign up for the Marines. By now I was seriously considering it.

We were talking at the office one morning and Staff Sergeant Lee said, *"Look Trent, you're not in school, you're not working, and you have no source of income coming in. Now you have the opportunity to join the most elite branch of service"*. Scott then said, *"Trent, we both ran track, and I know you can handle the challenge. The Marines would bring out the best in you"*. With those words from Scott and Staff Sergeant Lee, I was encouraged. Two days before Scott was to leave for his Military Occupational School for Training in December 1982, I made the decision to sign up for the United States Marine Corp.

There are only two places to go for Marine Corp Boot Camp. The west coast and Midwest recruits go to Marine Corp Recruit Depot San Diego, California, and the east coast recruits go to Marine Corp Recruit Depot, Parris Island, South Carolina. I signed up for the Delayed Entry Program, which is a program where you have completed all requirements to join the Marines. You have signed the dotted line and have been officially sworn in, but you are not immediately shipped out for Boot Camp until several months later. I had the opportunity to have lunch with my friend Scott before he departed for his Military Occupational School for Training. He advised me to run and exercise before leaving for Boot Camp. I ran and worked out almost every day until I shipped out for Marine Corp Boot Camp, San Diego California in April 1983.

Chapter 2

Marine Corp Boot Camp

I arrived at the Indianapolis International airport and boarded my plane. There were about a dozen Marine recruits on that same flight. I didn't know this until we arrived at the San Diego International airport and were directed on where to go by airport personnel. We were walking along introducing ourselves, laughing and joking. We went around the corner to an isolated area. There behind a desk sat a Marine Sergeant in uniform. We approached him and said, *"We're here for Marine Corp Boot Camp".* He looked up and shouted, "The first and last words out of your nasty mouths from now on will be Sir, yes Sir! Do you understand me? We responded, *"Ah, yeah, yes sir!"* I was thinking that we had not even arrived at the base but were still at the airport. He walked us outside, and there was about fifty more recruits standing silently at attention, in yellow footprints that were painted on the sidewalk outside of the airport in a designated area for Marine recruits going to Boot Camp. The Sergeant ordered us to stand in a set of empty footprints. As we were standing there waiting for the bus to pick us up, people were driving by laughing and cracking jokes, and saying things like *"Better you than me"* and *"Look at those idiots".* Finally about 1:00 a.m., the bus arrived. The bus driver was a Marine. We all got on the bus not saying a word. As we were driving, everyone was looking straight ahead. After about fifteen minutes of driving, we arrived at the main gate of the base.

At the front gate were two Marine military police that looked very sharp. Their green camouflaged fatigues were highly pressed, their boots were spit-shined, and they had black belts that were neatly centered around them with their .45 caliber pistols, ammunition pouches, and their PSH-24 side-handle batons snapped on their belts. They waved us through where we saw a red and scarlet gold sign that read "Marine Corp Recruit Depot, San Diego, California." It was now about 1:40 a.m., and we were driving down pitch dark roads. All of a sudden the bus driver looked at us in his rearview mirror and said in a Hispanic accent, *"You boys are going to have a long night"*.

It was so quiet on the bus that you could have heard a needle drop. The bus made a right turn, and we could see light up ahead about 300 meters. As we got closer, we could see three Marine Corp Drill Instructors with their hats, which are called Smokey's, low over their eyes. We were minutes away from beginning our journey through Marine Corp Boot Camp. I was thinking, *"It's about to begin"*.

As soon as he stopped the bus, one of the Drill Instructors came charging on the bus yelling, *"Get off the bus now!"* We were all bumping into each other trying to get off the bus. Then they ran us into the barracks and had us all stand at attention and began harassing us. After about 45 minutes of harassing us, they gave us hygiene bags and told us that everyone had to shave. I had never shaved in my life. I had a baby face with not one speck of hair on it. We were all in the 'head' (which is the bathroom) shaving, and I didn't know what I was doing. I cut my face in several places, and blood was all over the place. One of the Drill Instructors began questioning and yelling at me asking, *"You don't know how to shave boy?"* He began tearing into me.

It was about 6:00 a.m., and we were all tired and weary from being up without any sleep, from the time we arrived until now. Two of the Drill Instructors disappeared. The Drill Instructor that was left marched us to the chow hall for breakfast. After breakfast, we got haircuts. The civilian barbers sheared us bald in about 15 seconds. Afterwards, we were fitted for our uniforms, and all of our civilian clothes were boxed and stored away. We now had on camouflaged fatigues and boots. We were in what is called a receiving Platoon, where we have just one Drill Instructor. We remained in the receiving Platoon for two weeks, until we were picked up by our Drill Instructors who would train us for three months to earn the title **Marine**.

The day before we were to be picked up by our training Drill Instructors, I was anticipating what I was about to go through, the mental and physical challenge of the Drill Instructors trying to break you, but yet mold you into Marines, and I was hours away from finding out. We all tried to get a good night's sleep because we knew tomorrow, Boot Camp would begin. The next morning we woke up, marched to the chow hall and ate breakfast. After breakfast, our receiving Platoon Drill Instructor marched us to the barracks where we would be introduced to our Series Commander and our Drill Instructors, who would train us through a rigorous mental and physical challenging Boot Camp to earn the title **Marine**.

The receiving Drill Instructor called the Platoon to attention. Here we were, all of us sitting in what is called the classroom, and in walks our Series Commander, 1st Lieutenant T.J. Beaty. The series consisted of three

Platoons – 2037, 2038 and 2039. I was assigned to 2039. In each Platoon, there were about 65-75 recruits with four Drill Instructors assigned to each one. The Platoons were separated, and we lived in different living quarters called "squad bays". 1st Lieutenant Beaty welcomed each Platoon separately. He welcomed my Platoon, gave us words of encouragement, and then introduced us to our Senior Drill Instructor, Staff Sergeant J.J. Sixta. 1st Lieutenant Beaty left the barracks after he was done. Senior Drill Instructor Staff Sergeant Sixta gave us an introduction speech and told us what was expected of us while going through Marine Corp Boot Camp. After he finished his speech, he introduced the three Drill Instructors under him or as many would say, the three "pit bulls." Sergeant C.D. Brown, Sergeant T.E. Venable, and Corporal T. J. Andreasen. They come out of an office in the classroom that was called the Duty Hut, looking meaner than Tasmanian devils. As they came out of the Duty Hut, their movements were sharp and crisp, and the three of them centered themselves in front of the Platoon standing at attention. We were all scared stiff! Then the Senior Drill Instructor's next command was, *"Drill Instructors, they're all yours"*. The three pit bull Drill Instructors went into attack mode as the Senior Drill Instructor calmly walked into the Duty Hut. They were screaming, hollering, and yelling. It was total chaos. They started tearing bunk beds in the squad bay apart and told us, *"You got about a heartbeat to put them back together"*. Drill Instructor Sergeant Brown yelled out *"When I tell you to move from point A to point B, you better move and you better move fast. All I want to see is elbows and ass. Do you ladies understand me?"* We responded by saying, *"Sir, yes sir"*. Sergeant Brown then said *"Sound off with some bass in your voice. Do you ladies understand me?"*

Then we responded louder *"Sir Yes Sir"*. After that, the Drill Instructors placed us in four squads, from the tallest to the shortest. They chose four squad leaders and the Platoon Guide. We were then placed on line, which is when every recruit is standing at attention in front of our bunk beds with our bunk mates. The Drill Instructors began walking up and down the line randomly harassing recruits. Sergeant Venable stood in front of one recruit and said, *"Where you from boy?"* The recruit yelled out, *"Sir, I'm from Arizona but I was born and raised in Louisiana."* The Drill Instructor yelled back, *"Louisiana! Boy are you a swamp monster?"* The recruit yelled back, *"Sir, no sir."* The Drill Instructor yelled back, *"Son, you a freakin' liar, you a swamp monster that's been sliming around the swamps of Louisiana and now you're trying to sneak into my Marine Corp. I'll be keeping a close eye on you at night to make sure you're not sliming around at night trying to kill off my recruits."*

This was just the first day (training day one), and I sensed it was going to be a long three months. Why did I let Scott Rush talk me into this? On training day two, we had to fill out some paperwork providing information with our next of kin, phone number and address of who to contact in case of an emergency and other information. The Drill Instructors gave us three minutes to complete the paperwork, and told us to fill it out correctly and not to make any mistakes. One recruit ran up and handed his paperwork to the Drill Instructor who looked it over and found out that there were mistakes on it. He yelled at him while giving him another form saying, *"Go back and fill it out correctly"*. That same recruit came back up again with his completed form, the Drill Instructor looked it over and it was incorrect again. He looked at the recruit and said, *"I'll* be damned, you done messed up again son, that's two times, you done messed my paperwork up – three strikes, you out! That means you've got one last chance to get it right. If you come back up here a third time with my paperwork incorrect, my black combat boot is going to be so far up your butt, we both gonna have to go to the hospital to have it surgically removed". I was hoping he would get it right. When he came back up again, he was shaking like the scarecrow on the "Wizard of Oz". The Drill Instructor looked the paperwork over and said, "You're lucky son, now fall back in with the rest of the Platoon". After seeing that, I made a promise to myself that I was going to try to do everything correctly and to the best of my ability.

Boot Camp was broken down into three phases: First phase, second phase and third phase. We were taught and trained in various areas of military leadership, rifle, marksmanship, infantry tactics and weapons, hand-to-hand combat, rappelling, swim qualifications, physical fitness tests, the gas chamber, history of the Marine Corp, leadership traits and principles and more. The Drill Instructors were hard, but they were the best. They were going to make sure we were mentally and physically fit to serve in the United States Marine Corp.

Every morning, we would wake up to the trumpet sounding reveille and the Drill Instructor throwing the metal trash can down the squad bay yelling, "Get out your racks now and get dressed! Hurry up, hurry up, and do not be the one who gets caught still sleeping because you will definitely be in for a rude awakening". Every day was challenging when we ran PT (physical training). The series would start the morning by doing the daily seven which is seven exercises. Then we would go on a 2-6 mile formation run (no recruit would dare drop out of a run). The Series Commander, 1st Lieutenant Beaty, would lead the run. The Senior Drill Instructor would run up front next to the Series Commander. The other three Drill Instructors would position themselves throughout the Platoon. One would be on the left calling cadence; one would be on the right making sure everyone was sounding off; and one would be to the rear of the Platoon making sure no one fell back past him (which you did not want to do).

We were at the end of training day five of Boot Camp. Every night before we hit the sack, the duty Drill Instructor would conduct a hygiene inspection of the Platoon on line. He would check our shave, hands, and feet, and ask us if we had any personal or medical problems at this time. On this particular night, the duty Drill Instructor Sergeant Venable said to us *"I know some of y'all don't want to be here, that's fine with me; we'll send you back home. Tomorrow morning I will march you down to the administrative office, get your voluntary discharge papers typed up, get your plane tickets, and get you on a bus to the airport, it's that easy. At this time whoever don't want to be here, I need you to come forward".* Eight recruits ran up front and stood at attention. The Drill Instructor looked at them and said, *"Guess what ladies? I lied! I just needed to know who my mama's boys are".* Then he began yelling, *"I got your name, I got your number. So you want to go back home to mama, huh? So she can give you a bottle of milk, some Girl Scout Cookies, tuck you in bed and then tell you a bedtime story? YOU AIN'T GOING NOWHERE! I will motivate each one of you. You are my recruits; I will train you to the best of my ability. I will develop you into smartly, disciplined and physically* trained Marines, thoroughly indoctrinated in love of God, Country and Corps. I will demand of you and demonstrate by my own example, the highest standards of personal conduct, morality and professional skills. The road you will travel to get there won't be easy, but I will get you there. That I promise". He then thrashed them for twenty minutes, and then sent them to bed drenched in sweat. I was glad I did not go forward.

Every recruit has to have a determination deep within him to want to make it through Boot Camp and earn the title **Marine**. By the time second phase started, we lost nine recruits who were sent home because they couldn't hack it. Sundays were our best days because we had the opportunity to go to church. The Drill Instructors would tell us, *"It would be in your best interest to go to church to get a break from us, because if you don't, your hide is mine"*. I wanted to go to worship services, because I accepted Christ at a young age and my mother and father taught me the importance of serving God. But there were some recruits who were not spiritual, and even some who did not believe, but would go to church just to get away from the Drill Instructors.

As time went on, we were getting closer to graduation. We had finished qualifying on the rifle range and completed our field training on infantry tactics. The third and final phase of the Boot Camp had begun, and we were on home stretch. The only way I wouldn't make it now would be if I was injured. Graduation was knocking at our door. Our Platoon won the Initial Drill competition in first phase. This was a competition against Platoon 2037 and 2038, where each Platoon is graded on rifle and marching drill movements. When we were announced the winners, that was one of the few times I had seen the Drill Instructors smile. Now our Drill Instructors eyes were set on winning Final Phase Drill Competition against Platoon 2037 and 2038. We drilled everyday preparing for Final Phase Drill. Now with only one week before graduation, the Drill Instructors were still driving us hard in training, and they were not letting up, because we were still considered recruits who had not yet earned the title **Marine** until they officially announced it the day before graduation.

One day we were eating evening chow, and recruit Espinoza, who was a diet recruit because he was overweight when Boot Camp began, was limited to eating only salad, vegetables, grits, oatmeal, other light foods and drink water and juices. He had shed a lot of pounds and was doing very good. This particular day, he decided to sneak a cheeseburger from another recruit. Drill Instructor Sergeant Venable saw him out of the corner of his eye. As I was eating, I could see Sergeant Venable coming out of nowhere. He ran up on recruit Espinoza, and yelled out, *"You thought nobody was looking? You just want to sneak one of my cheeseburgers and feed your fat face, knowing you are on a restricted diet. Get outside now fat one! Matter of fact, everyone get outside now. You're done eating 2039. Thanks to recruit Espinoza, the whole Platoon is going to pay"*. We had only gotten a few mouthfuls of food. Sergeant Venable thrashed the whole Platoon outside. It was a lesson to everyone to not let our guards down.

It was now Tuesday 21 June (the final Drill Competition was Thursday 23 June), and graduation was Friday 24 June. We had completed all our requirements – rifle qualifications, swim qualifications, field training, gas chamber, all administrative tests, and our final physical fitness test. We were preparing to go on our last PT run of Boot Camp, which was a motivational beach run. All three Platoons in the series were lined up in formation 2037, 2038 and 2039. The series Chief Drill Instructor Gunnery Sergeant Green called the series to attention. He then gave us the command *"Right face", and* it was totally silent. Series Commander 1st Lieutenant T.J. Beaty took up his position in the front of the series. Gunnery Sergeant Green shouted out, *"This is your last run in Boot Camp, let's sound off and let the world hear us. Let your voices echo across the ocean; let all the population of San Diego, California hear you. Let them know that the Marines are here".* His next command was, *"Double Time, March!"* He started calling cadence, and we were shouting at the top of our lungs. After running about a mile, we came to the bridge that leads to the beach. We came over the bridge and into the sand. 1st Lieutenant T.J. Beaty led us close to the ocean, where the water was hitting our shoes as we sang cadence. Our voices echoed off the waves and winds coming off the ocean. This was a motivational run that we will never forget.

It was now Thursday 23 June, the day of Final Drill Competition. My Platoon, 2039, was looking good. Our camouflaged fatigues were highly pressed, and our boots had a mean spit shine on them. We were competing against 2037 and 2038, and they both were focused on beating us. The stage was set. All the Platoons were lined up on the parade deck. The judges consisted of Marine Corps Sergeant Majors, Master Sergeants, 1st Sergeants and Gunnery Sergeants. My Platoon was the last to go. I felt confident that we were ready and could win again. If we could pull it off, maybe our Drill Instructors would lighten up on us the day before graduation. Our Senior Drill Instructor Staff Sergeant J.J. Sixta took his position on the parade deck. He gave the Platoon the command *"Fall in"*.

The Platoon fell in at close interval. Staff Sergeant Sixta looked at his drill card. Every move he made was sharp and with precision. His uniform was crisp, and his Smokey laid low over his eyes. He called out each drill movement with his command Drill Instructor voice that echoed in our ears and was clearly understood. Our last drill movement was pass and review, in which the Platoon will pass the center of the parade deck where all of the Marine judges will be stationed. If we could nail this, we had a good chance of winning final drill. When the Platoon made a column left, the squad leaders were marching too fast, which caused the middle and the rear of the Platoon to try and catch up, which in turn caused the whole Platoons' alignment to be off. When Staff Sergeant Sixta gave the command "eyes right" as we were passing the podium, we all knew we had blown it. Platoon 2038 took the honors and captured final drill. We knew the Drill Instructors were pissed off.

When we got back to the squad bay, the Platoon was standing on line at attention. The Drill Instructors were just staring at us with these crazed looks. Sergeant Brown yelled out, *"You blew it! That's right ladies, you screwed it the hell up"*. They thrashed us for about 45 minutes. I was hoping the day before graduation would go smooth, but we got through it.

Later that evening after chow, Senior Drill Instructor Staff Sergeant Sixta gave us a motivational speech, while the other Drill Instructors were standing at parade rest. *"You worked hard, you earned it. You are now Marines".* It was an emotional moment. We stood there PROUDLY! *We Did It!*

Staff Sergeant Sixta read off our military occupational school one by one. Staff Sergeant Sixta read my name: *"Private LaLand, 0311 infantry".* We marched to the administrative building and received our orders, plane tickets, leave papers and check. When Friday came (that long awaited, graduation day), it was a beautiful, sunny day.

You could see all the families out there, and we were standing tall in our Summer Service Alphas uniform. After the graduation ceremony, Staff Sergeant Sixta gave us our last command. *"Platoon 2039, dismissed".* The Platoon took one step backwards and did an about face. Everyone yelled *"Oh-rah!"* You could never forget your Drill Instructors. I had the utmost respect for them (Senior Drill Instructor Staff Sergeant J.J. Sixta, Drill Instructors Sergeant C.D. Brown, Sergeant T.E. Venable and Corporal T.J. Andreason).

Boot Camp is over now, and I earned the title **Marine**. Now I was ready for a well-deserved 10-day leave period. There were buses and taxis waiting to take us to the airport. Each Marine would be flying back to their hometown to spend time with family and friends before going on to their Military Occupational School. As I was sitting in the airport in my uniform, I was reflecting back three months when I was at this same airport in civilian clothes with an afro, going to Boot Camp. Now, I'm here in uniform as a Marine with a fresh high-and-tight haircut. It felt good. I was different. I was mentally and physically tough, and I was in the best shape I'd ever been in. Now I was going home for 10 days to hang out with family and friends and tell them what Marine Corp Boot Camp was like.

I arrived in Indianapolis late Friday evening about 7 p.m. on 24 June 1983. My brother and sister were there to pick me up from the airport. When they saw me, they knew I was different. When I arrived at my parent's house, they gave me bear hugs and were so glad to see me. We ate, and I shared stories with my family about what Boot Camp was like. I met up with friends the next day. We hung out for a while. After a mentally and physically challenging Boot Camp, I was enjoying every moment of my 10-day leave period. The time went by quickly. Now, I was here saying goodbye to my family and friends before going to the airport to fly to my Military Occupational School/Infantry Training School in Camp Pendleton, California. It was good to know that this time when I would fly to California it would not be for Boot Camp, but by no means was Infantry Training School going to be a cake walk.

SECOND BATTALION
PLATOON 2039

Commenced Training:
13 April 1983

Graduated:
24 June 1983

LtCol. C. R. Stichter, II
Battalion Commander

SgtMaj. M. C. Allen
Sergeant Major

Capt. M. A. Kachilla
C. O. Co. G

Maj. A. W. Spittler, II
Executive Officer

1stLt. J. P. Ford
Company Executive Officer

NOT PICTURED
1stSgt. A. Williams
Company First Sergeant

1stLt. T. J. Beaty
Series Commander

NOT PICTURED:
1stLt. J. D. Provenzano, III
Assistant Series Commander

GySgt S. A. Green
Series Chief DI

Pfc. F. S. Gomez
Platoon Honorman
Series Honorman

SSgt. J. J. Sixta
Senior Drill Instructor

Sgt. C. D. Brown
Drill Instructor

Sgt. T. E. Venable
Drill Instructor

Cpl. T. J. Andreasen
Drill Instructor

Chapter 3

Infantry Training School

I arrived in California on a Thursday afternoon. There were buses at the airport to take all Marines to Camp Pendleton. When we arrived at the Infantry Training School, we immediately went to the Admin Office to check in. There were Marines who went through Boot Camp at MCRD Parris Island, South Carolina and MCRD San Diego, California. The check-in process took two days. Every Marine was checked in by 1500 hrs on Friday. Training would commence on Monday. We were given liberty call at 1530 hrs, and we had to be back at the barracks on Sunday at 1800 hrs. We were briefed by the company 1st Sergeant on the do's and don'ts for every Marine who was going in town to Oceanside, California. We had to use the buddy system where there were two or more Marines together at all times. I hooked up with three Marines that were in my Platoon in Boot Camp. We all showered up, got dressed and headed out to town by way of the bus. When we got off the bus in Oceanside, all we could see were jarheads...those Marines with that distinguished look and haircuts.

Private James Clemons and Private Robert Bryant wanted to get tattoos, so we stopped in a tattoo shop. Clemons had a USMC with a bulldog tattooed on his shoulder. Bryant had a USMC tattooed on his bicep. Afterwards, we walked down to the beach. There were Marines surfing, riding wave runners and hanging out with their girlfriends. I thought, *"So this is Marine Corp life* when we're not training". This was alright with me. We stopped at an outside café and ordered some food and beer. Later that night, we went to a club and partied. We arrived back at base around 0230 hrs. On Saturday, we went back to Oceanside and followed the same routine as the day before, minus the tattoos. Sunday we stayed on base, played basketball, and went to see a movie at the base theater. Later that day, we had a company formation in our camouflaged fatigues at 1800 hrs. There were over 150 Marines assigned to Bravo Company. Everyone was accounted for. There was not one Unauthorized Absence. The company 1st Sergeant told us that training would commence tomorrow, and there would be a company formation at 0530 hrs. We would march over to the armory to get our weapons, and there would be another formation at 0700 hrs with our rifle, pack, helmet and H-Harness.

Reveille would be at 0430 hrs. He called the company to attention and yelled out, "Bravo Company, dismissed". We were not allowed to go back in town or off base. We stayed in the barracks, talked and played cards. Some Marines made phone calls at the phone booth area near the barracks. I stayed up for a little while, but I hit the rack early because I knew 0430 hrs would come fast. I was getting ready to start the second phase of my stint in the Marine Corp, Infantry Training School. The school would last for 30 days and was designed to prepare Marines before being assigned to a Marine Infantry Battalion in the Fleet Marine Force (FMF). We would be thoroughly trained in infantry tactics, patrolling, ambushes, booby traps, setting up claymore mines, land navigations, map orientation, and learning to fire and operate various weapons such as the M203 grenade launcher, M60 machine gun, m50 caliber machine gun, hand grenades and the LAW (Light Anti-tank Weapon).

When 0430 hrs came, we got up, went to the chow hall and ate a good, hot breakfast. Afterwards, we marched to the armory, got our weapons and were in formation at 0700 hrs standing tall with our rifles and packs, ready for our first day of training. In all, we had 14 instructors consisting of Non-Commissioned Officers and Staff Non-Commissioned Officers, one Company Commander, a Captain and one Executive Officer (a 1st Lieutenant). Most of our training would be conducted in the field, but we would also have classroom training, several PT runs, two hikes and a physical fitness test. The instructors were very professional, thorough, and knew their stuff. Every Friday about 1900 hrs, we would secure for liberty call. We had to be back at the barracks on Sunday at 1800 hrs, in uniform for formation. The last week of school, each Marine would find out what unit he would be assigned to in the Fleet Marine Force. Some Marines would be assigned to special duty, such as Marine Barracks duty or Sea duty on a Navy aircraft carrier, but everyone else would be assigned to a Marine Corp Infantry Battalion.

We were all motivated and ready to be a part of the Fleet Marine Force. Friday, 31 August, would be graduation. On Friday 24 August, we had trained hard all day round the clock, and we were dead tired. The instructors told us that motor transport was sending five-ton trucks to pick us up and take us back to the barracks. We would turn our weapons in to the armory, go to the chow hall and get a hot meal, then secure for liberty around 1930 hrs. It was 1715 hrs, and the company was standing at the modified position of parade rest with our packs and rifles. The company Gunnery Sergeant walked out and said, *"Guess what, gents? The five-ton trucks are not coming to pick us up, but transportation has already arrived. Every Marine, look down at your boots. Those black Cadillac's are going to get us to our destination"*. We already knew what time it was. His next command was, *"Bravo Company, Uh –Ten-Hut, Right Face, Port Arms, Double Time, MARCH!"* The Gunny began calling cadence, *"Ah Recon Shuffle"*. As tired as we were, we were sounding off loud, covered and aligned, and in step. The run was about three and a half miles. We were so glad when we saw the barracks. The Chow Hall stayed open late to feed us. After chow, we had a company formation, and the company Gunnery Sergeant told us that on Monday 27 August we would find out which units we would be assigned to in the Fleet Marine Force (FMF) and which Marines would be assigned to special duty. About 1945 hrs, liberty was sounded. This would be our last weekend at the school.

After liberty call was sounded, I stayed in the barracks, took a shower and relaxed. Saturday I went in to town for a little while, and on Sunday I played basketball and went to the movies at the base theater.

When Monday came, we were standing tall with rifles and packs at 0700 hrs ready to roll. Our instructors would tell us, *"The more you sweat in peacetime, the less you bleed in combat"*, meaning U.S. Marines focus on being physically fit and conditioned, able to fight in every climate and place whether it is in the jungle, desert, mountainous environment or cold weather, snow…Marines are mentally and physically prepared to fight anywhere in the world, and that training is not designed to be easy, but is designed to prepare Marines to fight in prolonged, harsh and difficult conditions. They talked to us about the harsh conditions Marines endured during WWII against the Japanese in the Island Hopping campaigns. Those Marines would go from island to island, fighting in thick dense, snake-infested jungles against a well dug-in Japanese Army that was ordered to fight until their deaths. Heat, malaria, tropical diseases, and jungle rot became the Marines enemy too. After the US Marines would defeat the Japanese on one island, they would embark back on US Navy ships and prepare to attack another island, such as Pelilulu, the Solomon Islands, Saipan, Guam, Okinawa, Tarawa, and Iwo Jima.

We also learned US Marines can be called into action to go into any country in the world at a moment's notice without the act of Congress. The first part of the day we would be training on live fire ranges, and the second part of the day, we would be conducting infantry tactics on the squad level. Later that evening after training, Bravo Company was assembled in the barracks at 1900 hrs. The company gunny came out with a list and began reading off our orders. The majority of the Marines were being sent to different Marine Infantry Battalions at 1st Marine Division Camp Pendleton, California and some 2nd Marine Division Camp Lejeune, North Carolina. There were a few Marines who were hand-picked for Recon Battalions at 1st and 2nd Marine Divisions. These were special units who worked behind enemy lines to gather intelligence for Marine Infantry Units who would later attack the enemy. Marine Recon Unit's motto is: Swift, Silent and Deadly.

My name was finally called – 'Private LaLand, Marine Barracks Duty, Subic Bay, Philippines'. One of the instructors, Sergeant Blake, said *"What? You got barracks duty Philippines? You gonna have to show me something Private LaLand"*. I thought, this Sergeant acts like I just won the lottery. The next day when we were in the field, one of the instructors talked to me about the Philippines. He said that it is one of the best duty stations you can get in the Marines.

They call it Paradise Island. There were just two of us who got orders for the Philippines – me and another Marine named Private James Frechetti. Immediately after graduation on Friday, we would fly out of California to the Philippines. The last three days of school went by smoothly. On Thursday 30 August, we spent the day cleaning up the barracks, packing our gear, and preparing for graduation. We graduated Friday, 31 August 1983. After graduation, we said our goodbyes to each other, and every Marine was off to their duty stations.

UNITED STATES MARINE CORPS
Company "B"
Marine Barracks, Subic Bay
Box 17, FPO San Francisco, CA 96654

7 September 1983

Mr. and Mrs. Rudolph Laland
2531 Boulevard Place
Indianapolis, IN 46208

Dear Mr. and Mrs. Laland,

Your son has recently joined my command and has been assigned to work for me as
a security guard. I would like to take this opportunity to tell you about
Trent's new assignment.

Company "B" is located at U. S. Naval Air Station, Cubi Point, Republic of the
Philippines. The Company is organized into a headquarters platoon comprised of
company headquarters personnel and a security section comprised of three
security platoons. The assigned mission of Company "B" is to provide security
for the Naval Air Station and the Naval Magazine in coordination with other
security elements. This includes manning of the thirty-two posts within the
Naval Magazine and other sensitive areas. Here we enforce entry and exit
procedures to prevent unauthorized entry, the removal of unauthorized material
or government property from the Naval Magazine. In addition we conduct jungle
patrols daily to apprehend intruders in the huge magazine.

During your son's tour here he will stand duty at all security posts. The
facilities aboard the base are more than adequate to meet your son's needs.

The Naval Facility here at Subic Bay has one of the finest recreational
facilities available on any military base. We have two libraries, three
swimming pools, horseback riding, a skeet range, archery, sailing, scuba diving,
flying, four beaches, five movie theaters, five athletic fields, and even a
go-cart track. In addition to these facilities your son has available high
school level and college level courses taught by highly qualified civilian
instructors.

In spite of the outstanding facilities available, duty in the company is
considered demanding duty. Your son has been specifically screened and selected
for this special assignment. His duties demand a high degree of responsibility
and extraordinary reliability. This will be a trying and difficult job
involving many long, hard hours. You can help by writing him frequently and
keeping him informed of the good news at home. Small packages and letters from
home go a long way towards keeping a Marine's morale high and reducing the
loneliness of tour in a foreign land.

If I may be of assistance to you at anytime during your son's tour please feel
free to contact me.

                              Sincerely yours,

                              W. A. LACHAPELLE
                              Major, U. S. Marine Corps
                              Commanding

Chapter 4

First Assignment – Philippines

Private Frechetti and I caught a military flight to the Philippines. It was a long flight. We touched down at Clark Air Force Base, Philippines about 1800 hrs. After we grabbed our sea bags and clothing bags, we rode a Filipino jeepney all the way to headquarters, Marine Barracks Subic Bay. It was about a two-hour ride, and it was a totally different atmosphere. It was like being in a different world. You saw all these Filipino vendors on the sidewalk selling food, souvenirs, pictures, jewelry…just about everything. Taxis were three-wheeled motorcycles with a cab attached that could carry about four people. Private Frechetti and I just observed in awe…two Marines fresh in the Corps, getting stationed in a foreign land. We arrived at headquarters Marine Barracks Subic Bay at 2000 hrs. We checked in with the duty staff non-commissioned officer. We were both assigned to Bravo Company. They were located at Cubi Point, about a twenty-minute drive from Subic Bay. Headquarters and Alpha Company were based at Subic Bay and Charlie Company was in the boonies. We were taken to Bravo Company by the Marine Headquarters vehicle. When we arrived at Bravo Company, we checked in with the duty officer. Both of us were assigned to 3rd Platoon port side. We received our room keys and linen. Our Platoon was on a 96-hour pass, which is four days off, and they were having a section party in the town right outside the main gate called Olongapo City at a open café bar called The 168.

The word was already out to the Platoon that two boot newbie's fresh out of Infantry Training School, had checked in to the Platoon. When the duty officer walked us over to the barracks, there was a Marine Lance Corporal from our Platoon dressed in civilian clothes with a Bravo Company shirt on waiting to take us out into town to meet our Platoon. He gave us both Bravo Company shirts to put on. We took a quick shower, changed into civilian clothes, and caught a cab from the barracks. The cab dropped us off at the main gate, which Alpha Company guards. You walk from there to the town Olongapo City. It was only a five-minute walk to bar 168, and as soon as the Platoon saw us, they began hollering and yelling *"Get over here newbie's"*. They sat us down at a table and asked us *"Do you drink?"* We were like *"A little bit"*. They said *"Try this for starts"*. They slammed down these 16 oz bottles of beer called Red Horse. Private Frechetti and I started drinking these beers, and they were strong. After drinking two of them, I had a buzz. Then they slammed this tropical-colored fruity drink down on the table called Mo Joe, and said *"Try some of this"*. It was fruity, sweet and good, but it was full of gin and vodka. They had a variety of food spread out on two tables. I was hungry and started scarfing it down. After the section party was over, we began club hopping. There were clubs lined up on both sides of the street – disco, country western, heavy metal and rock & roll. The whole Platoon would roll into the club with our Marine Barracks Bravo Company shirts on. All the Filipino girls yelled, *"It's Bravo Company"*. I said to my self, *"Bravo Company has a serious reputation"*. We would hit the dance floor, drink some more, and after about thirty minutes, we would go to the next club. We did this all night. I was intoxicated. I've never drank that much. Two Marines from the Platoon escorted me back to base. We walked from town to the main gate. When you get to the main gate, you have to show your I.D. to get on base. I was staggering a little bit, and fumbling to get my I.D. out. There were Marine guards from Alpha Company and Filipino guards who man that gate 24/7, to ensure no intruders gain access to the base. We caught a cab back to Cubi Point. They walked me to my room and put me in my bed. I was out for the count.

The next morning, I woke up with a serious hangover. I met my two roommates, Lance Corporal Bryan Kortech, and Lance Corporal Willie Manning. I was then introduced to my team leader Lance Corporal Brent Harwood who was a body-builder. I was definitely not going to get on his bad side. It was Saturday, and we didn't have to be back at work until Tuesday morning. My team leader and my roommates took me to the chow hall to eat, and then introduced me to my Filipino houseboy whose name was Rudy. Each Marine was assigned a houseboy. They washed our laundry, pressed our camouflaged fatigues, and spit-shined our boots, as well as other tasks. We would pay them every payday. I thought calling them houseboys was disrespectful. They were grown men who had wives and families. This is how they made their living. They should be called "house men". Afterwards, they gave me a tour of the base, and then the Town of Olongapo. The Philippines was a beautiful tropical island surrounded by jungle and water. Now I see why my instructor from Infantry Training School said they call it Paradise Island. There was so much to do there; snorkeling, scuba diving, chartering boats to go deep-sea fishing, visiting different islands, going to Manila the capital of the Philippines, shopping and so much more… I had an awesome time on my four days off.

When Tuesday came, Private Frechetti and I had to go do mandatory In-doctrine Training for three days learning about the Philippines, their culture, what to expect, what to be careful of while in town, and the dos and don'ts and what the base has to offer. One of the things that were highly emphasized during the first day of In-Doc Training was to be aware of the monkeys, because they were very aggressive.

Marines from Bravo Company Subic Bay Philippines having a good time at night. Courtesy: Trent LaLand

My Platoon was assigned to guard the US Naval magazine and conduct routine jungle patrols, to ensure no intruders were trespassing. The Naval magazine was located in an isolated area surrounded by the country's thick dense jungle. Within the magazine, we had five posts to guard, Papa Oscar 1,2,3,6, and Mike 1. Each post, except Mike 1, had these large reinforced concrete magazines that concealed sophisticated US weapons and equipment in them. Each post was a one-man post, except Papa Oscar 3, which were two Marines, one in the tower and one on foot patrol. Mike 1 was the main gate that leads into the Naval magazines. The Marine on guard there stood that post in modified dress blues, with a .45 caliber pistol. There were three shifts, 8-12, 12-4, and 4-8 from Tuesday to Tuesday. After our seven days of duty was complete, we were relieved by 3rd Platoon Starboard Side.

Every Marine had a top-secret clearance that was documented in our service record book. Each day after completing In-Doctrine training, Private Frechetti and I would be picked up by the Corporal of the guard and taken to the naval magazine. Corporal Gallagher, who was one of the Corporals of the Guards for our Platoon, gave us a tour of the magazine each day, showing us each post that we would be guarding, and to get us familiarized with the naval magazine and our job description. He explained to us that during the Monsoon season, when it rains almost non-stop creating floods, we were to bring extra sets of camouflaged fatigues, because we would get very wet standing post. When we conduct jungle patrols, there will be a Filipino scout that would accompany us. We also would have to be very alert, not for just intruders, but dangerous reptiles, particularly snakes. Corporal Gallagher said that one Marine patrol captured a large python, and one Marine killed a poisonous snake that was crawling towards him with the butt of his M-16 rifle. The snake was a viper, and it was green with a diamond-shaped head. If he had been bitten, he would have died within minutes.

It was now close to 1800 hrs. We were driving to the chow hall in the magazine to get a bite to eat before they closed. As we were driving down the road, you could see the monkeys in the trees and on the sides of the roads. Corporal Gallagher warned us that the monkeys are very aggressive, which we had already been told in our First day of In-Doctrine training. He told us that when we come out of the chow hall, do not have any food in your hand because the monkeys will attack you for it. When you throw trash in the dumpster, do not open the sliding door with your body exposed to the opening, but move to the side as you open the door, because there might be five or more monkeys in the dumpster scavenging for food. If your body is exposed to the opening and you surprise them, it is a very good chance that they will attack you. I said *"Man, these monkeys must be some bad dudes"*, and we all started laughing.

The chow hall in the naval magazine was a very small building that was run by one Filipino cook and one Filipino dishwasher. After we ate chow, we drove back to the guard shack. Private Frechetti and I would start standing duty the next day, Saturday, the 12-4 shift. I was assigned Papa Oscar 6 and Private Frechetti to Papa Oscar 2. All newbie's were assigned to the worst shift, 12-4. It was the hottest time of the day, and it is known as the graveyard shift at night. That night on post, I will admit I was scared. I could hear things moving in the jungle and all kinds of weird noises. After a month of standing duty, you get used to it. One time, I was standing duty on Papa Oscar 3, which is the two-man post. This particular day, I was the Marine who was patrolling on foot. I stood in a small eight foot booth on post to take a break from the sun, and to get a drink of water. When I came out of the booth, I walked a few feet and turned around. There was a monkey on top of the booth. I didn't even hear when it climbed over the fence. I looked at him as he looked at me. He hunched his back up, his teeth came out and he jumped down and started to chase me. After about 20 meters, he stopped chasing me, jumped the fence, and darted back into the jungle. I was thinking, if he did catch up to me, I was going to beat him with the butt of my M-16 rifle. We were taught that before we could use deadly force, it had to be a life or death situation. If a Marine were to use deadly force and it was determined after an investigation that it was not justified, he would be subjected to punishment by the uniform code of the Military Justice.

When we arrived back at the guard shack after duty, Private Thomas, who was in the tower, told the rest of the Platoon that a monkey came on post and chased me. Everyone fell out laughing. They dogged me out all week about it. I said *"that's okay, y'all can dog me out but I wasn't trying to get bit by this vicious monkey"*. Monkeys carry viruses, and if you get bitten by one, you could get infected. Overall, the duty was great once you got the hang of everything. Everyone liked the routine of standing seven straight days on guard duty in the naval magazine, and then rotating out for seven days.

Every new Marine was also required to go through JEST (Jungle Environmental Survival Training) School. When you go through JEST School, you do not take any MRE's (meals ready to eat) with you. It's complete survival. This training teaches Marines how to survive in a jungle environment without being re-supplied by food or water for a prolonged period of time. Once you complete the school, you receive a certificate of completion. Private Frechetti and I were still considered boot newbies, even though we had stood duty, completed JEST School and been on jungle patrols. But it didn't matter, because we loved our First duty station in the Marines. You couldn't get bored on this tropical island, because there was so much to do. When we were off duty, there was a popular club in town where Marines from Alpha Company, Bravo Company, and a US Navy Seal team that was based in the Philippines would party at. There were also the most beautiful American and Filipino women who would socialize at this club as well. They loved Marines and Navy Seals. It started to become a territorial battle between the Marines and Navy Seals. The Marines would wear their Alpha and Bravo Company shirts. The Seal team would wear their beige UDT shorts and Navy blue shirts, with the Seal emblem on them. A good portion of the Marines from Alpha and Bravo Company were body-builders, including my Team Leader Lance Corporal Harwood. All of the Navy Seals were also body- builders. The Marines would start to get rowdy after drinking. Things would then turn into a verbal confrontation between Marines and Seals, which eventually led to a physical altercation. Shore Patrol Police were called to this club on many occasions to break up the fights between the Marines and Navy Seals. Word got back to the Senior Marine Base Commander, Colonel John Bowers, about the situation. He made the decision to make the club off limits to the Marines, but the Navy Seals were allowed to continue going to that club. All the Marines were upset and figured the decision was made because it was a Naval Base.

My First tour of duty in the Marine Corp was awesome, and being stationed in the Philippines was a great adventure and experience. One month before I was to rotate back to the states, I received my orders for 2nd Battalion 5th Marines 1st Marine Division, Camp Pendleton, California. I flew out of the Philippines in November 1984 to go back to Indianapolis for a 30-day leave period before going to my next duty station. When I arrived home, my family was happy to see me, especially my mother. I spent most of my time with family and friends, telling stories about the Philippines, what it was like, and sharing pictures with them. When I told them about the monkey that chased me, they got a laugh out of that. As always, it was great to spend time with family and friends, but then the time comes when you have to say good-bye and head back to duty. You definitely miss them when you leave and the time you spend and share together, but everyone understands the commitment you made to the Military. My mother encouraged me to stay in contact with the family and attend church.

Department of the Navy

Certificate **of** *Training*

This is to certify that

PFC Trent R. LaLand

has satisfactorily completed the course of
24 HOUR (C-2B-0034)
JUNGLE ENVIRONMENTAL SURVIVAL TRAINING (JEST)

given at

Detachment U.S. Naval Air Station, Cubi Point, Philippines

Fleet Aviation Specialized Operational Training Group, Pacific Fleet

27 October 19 83

R. H. ROBERTS, LT., OIC, USN

Chapter 5

The Grunts

Well, here I am for my third stint of the Marine Corp the Grunts! Marine Grunts are known as the backbone of the Marine Corp, a force in readiness that can be called into action at a moment's notice. I arrived at Camp Pendleton, California in the first week of December 1984.

I was assigned to Golf Company 2nd Platoon. The 5th Marines were located at Camp Margarita. They call it the regiment on the hill, because the unit was based on a steep hill. Also on the hill was 1st Battalion 5th Marines and 3rd Battalion 5th Marines. The 1st Marines were located down in the Valley at Camp Horno. The 7th Marines were located at Camp San Mateo, and Force Recon Company was located in the boonies at Camp Talega.

When I checked into Golf Company, the company office was a Quonset hut surrounded by beautiful landscape. The Quonset huts seen in the 5th Marine regiment area were small horseshoe-shaped steel buildings that were from the WWII, Korea and Vietnam era. I met my Company 1st Sergeant Victor Slate, who was a Vietnam veteran. He was tall with broad shoulders. He looked hard as iron. He said, *"You are now a member of one of the most decorated Marine Infantry Regiments who proudly wear the French Fortejeh"*. This was awarded to the 5th and 6th Marine Regiments by the French in WWI for their brave and fierce fighting against the Germans in

France. He handed me my Fortejeh and then shook my hand and said, *"Welcome to the 5th Marines"*. He walked me over to meet my Platoon Commander, 2nd Lieutenant Robert Kahn and my Platoon Sergeant, Staff Sergeant James Darnell. They briefed me and let me know that our Battalion would be going on a six-month deployment in five months, and that we would be doing a lot of training leading up to the deployment.   My Platoon Sergeant walked me over to the squad bay to meet my Squad Leader, Sergeant Chad Cobbins, and the rest of my Platoon. As we walked into the Squad Bay, everyone was saying welcome to the Grunts. I met my Squad Leader and the rest of the Platoon one by one. Lance Corporal Don Childrey stuck out like a sore thumb. He was about 6 foot 8, towering over the whole Platoon. He shouted out *"How do you like your new home where you get to listen to everybody's music? Soul, country, rock & roll, heavy metal, and you get to share the same bathroom and shower"*. This definitely was a change for me. In the Philippines, I enjoyed living in the Barracks where we had nice plush rooms with carpet. Then the Marines from the Platoon began to tell me that we had a crazy Battalion Commander who they nicknamed 'Killer Kiley'. And of course I asked, *"Why is that?"* They said, *"He's mean as hell, and when we go on Battalion runs, we run eight miles or more. And our Battalion hikes are always thirty miles and up with full gear. He expects no one to drop out, and his expectations are high. Every Marine and Navy personnel that serve under him will be in top physical condition"*.

Each Marine Rifle Company was assigned, five Navy Corpsman, – one to each of the four Platoons, and one Senior Navy Corpsman. They were required to stay up on the runs and hikes, train with us on field operations, and deploy with us overseas. If we go into combat, these are the guys that patch us up if we are wounded. If a Navy Corpsman is wounded in a combat zone, the Marines are trained to give first-aid as well. Most Navy Corpsman were not used to the rigorous physical training that Marine grunts go through, and for some it was a rude awakening. Some were gung ho and okay with it, and some would say 'I didn't enlist in the Marines, I enlisted in the Navy', but most Navy Corpsman were able to adjust and develop a great relationship with the Marines.

As time moved on, I became closer to the Marines in my Platoon. We were just like brothers. Even though there were Marines of different races in the Platoon, we were all one color, green! Yea, green, mean fighting machines. We were a band of brothers. Everything the Marines from my Platoon told me when I checked in was true, not that I doubted them. The Battalion runs were 8 miles and up, and the Battalion hikes were over 30 miles with full gear. When we lined up in formation for the runs and the hikes, we were always last in formation, because they went in alphabetical order. Headquarters and Service Company was always first, then Weapons Company, Echo Company, Fox Company, and then Golf Company.

One Friday we had an eight-mile Battalion run. Our Company Commander Captain Timothy Swindle told Golf Company while we stood in formation before the run that *"if you let a forty-something-year-old man outrun you, then something is wrong"*. He was speaking of our Battalion Commander Lieutenant Colonel Kiley. Then he yelled out, *"Nobody drops out Golf Company"*. When you are the last company in Formation on a Battalion run with over 600 Marines and Navy personnel, you are sprinting half the time. As the Battalion came back up the hill that leads into

Camp Margarita, we started chanting *"Golf Company 2/5"*. When we finished, no one from our company dropped out. Our five Navy Corpsmen even made it. After each Battalion hike and run, we would have a Battalion formation where each Company Commander would give the Battalion Commander an accountability report of how many drop outs they had. This was the way he evaluated each Commander's ability to keep their Marines and Navy personnel in top physical condition. The Battalion was standing tall and at attention. The Battalion Commander and Battalion Sergeant Major were standing out in front of the Battalion. The Battalion Sergeant Major barked out with a command voice, *"Report"*. Lieutenant Colonel Kiley looked at each Commander as they give their report. H&S, Weapons, Echo and Fox Companies reported dropouts. When Golf Company reported, Captain Swindle proudly shouted out *"Golf Company, no drop outs"*. Lieutenant Colonel Kiley said, *"From now on Captain Swindle, your company will be the lead company on the runs and hikes"*.

Captain Swindle came to be Lieutenant Colonel Kiley's favorite company commander. We continued to build up for our upcoming six-month deployment overseas. I was looking forward to my first deployment with the grunts. The time came when we started to pack up and handle any legal matters, such as last will and testaments, just in case we passed away while on deployment; service record books, medical and dental records were updated; motorcycles, jet skis, and other personal belongings of unmarried Marines were put into storage units. Tradition has it that the day before deployment, Marines go get drunk. My Platoon hit the package store on base hard. We bought liquor and dozens of cases of beer. We were hung over and dragging the next morning in formation. We marched to the Armory to get our weapons, and when we arrived back to the battalion area, the buses were there to take us to the El Toro Marine Air Station where we would fly out on a Military flight to Okinawa, Japan. It was about a twelve -hour flight with a brief stop in Alaska.

We landed in the evening at Kadena Air Force Base in Okinawa, Japan. There were military buses waiting when we arrived to take us to Camp Hansen, where our Battalion would be based. The bus drive to Camp Hansen took about one hour. Once we arrived, we grabbed our sea bags and the rest of our gear, and settled in the squad bays where we would be living. We turned our weapons in at the armory, and the rest of the day was pretty laid back. We were not allowed to go out in town, but we were able to get familiar with Camp Hansen and, of course, we found out all the locations where we could get beer and liquor.

The next morning, we had a company formation at 0730 hrs. Captain Swindle came out and briefed us on the training exercises and the locations where we would be training for the next six months. We would be conducting jungle training in Japan at an area called NTA (Northern Training Area). We would be going to South Korea for two months of training, and that included us going through mountain warfare school which was run by South Korean Marines which are known as "Rock Marines". Our company was the only one chosen to go to a US Naval Base on Diego Garcia Island to cross-train with British Royal Marines. Diego Garcia is a small tropical island located in the middle of the Indian Ocean. We would also have our normal routine of physical training, Platoon runs, company runs, and hikes with full gear. Captain Swindle also made it known that it is mandatory that when we go out in town in Japan, or anywhere for liberty, that we use the buddy system: two or more Marines together at all times. He warned us that Japanese police, who are called (JP's), patrol on foot in town in groups of ten or more and they all know Karate. They target Marines, because they know Marines like to get drunk and wild. If a Marine gets disorderly and out of control, JP's will gang up on you and beat you down with their night sticks. Once you start to fight back, they will pull their guns on you. Our commanders knew that we were going to get drunk and wild, but we were told to use wisdom and good judgment. The last thing we would want, which has happened with Marine units in the past is having our commander bail us out of a Japanese jail where we would be under there jurisdiction. The goal is not to have any American incidents in town or wherever we have liberty call.

The first few days in town went well. There were no incidents. We went on our first training operation at NTA. This training was run by Marine instructors and was conducted on the squad and fire team level. We went through a brief instructional period to get us familiar with what we may encounter while in the jungle, what to do if you get lost or disoriented, and other important issues. One thing that was emphasized was the snakes that you may encounter. The instructors had live snakes that were caught in the jungle to show us. One of them was real hideous looking. The fangs in his mouth were so inverted that if it bites you, it would latch and stick onto you. Every Marine had to be alert while in the jungle. These snakes can easily camouflage in with the foliage. We were also told to watch out for wild boars.

The training was very good for squad leaders and fire team leaders to hone their skills in a jungle environment on day and night land navigation, map orientation, plotting, reconnaissance and compass reading. All squads from each Platoon were given ten check points to find using different starting points. The grid coordinates were six-to-eight digit grids. The squad leaders and fire team leaders worked together to plot their grid coordinates and azimuths on laminated maps for each check point. If your squad got lost or disoriented, there was an escape azimuth you shoot with your compass that would bring you out of the jungle and back on the main road. When the squads came out of the jungle after going through the night land navigation course, they reported to the Company Commander Captain Swindle. If you didn't find all of your checkpoints, he would make your squad go back in the jungle, and he would tell the squad leader *"Don't come back out until you have found all your check points"*. Captain Swindle was hard on the NCOs. He made sure that all NCOs were fully knowledgeable in all areas of infantry tactics and skills and were able to lead their men in combat. After we finished our training at NTA, our battalion would fly out of Japan to South Korea for two months for our next training exercises.

It was a great experience to see different cultures and how they live. We were told that we would get liberty call in Pohang and Seoul, Korea, and that the shops for souvenirs and clothing had remarkable bargains, but training would come first.

When we were not in the field training, our battalion stayed at Camp Muchuk, which was also called 'tent city'; nothing but rows and rows of tents. We slept on cots that were already in the tents, and each tent had heaters in them. Korea would get very cold, especially at night where it would get into the single digits and sometimes below zero during the winter months. There were tents that were designated as bathrooms with homemade toilets in them made out of wood. A lot of Marines kept Coke bottles by their cots at night to urinate in, because they didn't want to get out of a warm sleeping bag, get dressed and walk about a block to the bathroom.

Our battalions first training exercise in South Korea was going through the "Rock Marines" rugged 10-day Mountain Warfare School Course.

Lance Corporal Martinez Golf Company 2/5 2nd platoon in a two man Foxhole South Korea. Courtesy: Trent LaLand

Lance Corporal Sumpter, Golf Company 2/5 1st Platoon in wrestling match with an South Korean Marine. Courtesy: Trent LaLand

Lance Corporal Trent LaLand with young Korean children in Seoul Korea. Courtesy: Trent LaLand

Lance Corporal LaLand, singing karaoke at a local club in Seoul Korea. Courtesy: Trent LaLand

The South Korean Marine Colonel along with his instructors welcomed our battalion and briefly talked to us about the school and the course we would be going through. We started the course the same day we arrived. The instructors were very professional. The training was challenging and awesome. We learned how to fight in a mountainous environment. We did everything from scaling cliffs, cliff assaults, and river crossing from a roped bridge, rappelling, and Australian rappelling down the side of the mountain. There were seven lanes for the Australian rappelling down the mountain that Marines were assigned to. The Korean Marines ensured that each US Marine was correctly snapped into each line of rope. Once that happened, the instructor gave the word to go. Each Marine went down his lane face first (Australian Rappell), feet touching the mountain. You are actually running down the mountain until you reach the bottom where you are disconnected, then run to your next station. The rotation at the top of the mountain keeps going where the next seven

Marines are snapped into their lines of rope. Everything is like clockwork. Training is around the clock, it doesn't stop until we are finished. Another challenging station at the school was 'Australian Rappelling off the hell hole'. This was a small platform suspended 300 feet in the air that you would Australian Rappell from. The fun part was getting to the platform. There was a 75-foot long, two-strand roped bridge that came out from the mountain that you had to walk across before you arrived at the platform. When I went, there were four of us walking across the bridge at the same time. You had to fight to keep your balance as you moved forward, crossing your boots in front of each other and disconnecting and connecting your safety ring to move past each sector of rope. If you did lose your balance and fall, your safety line kept you suspended in air until you could get back on the roped bridge. If you hesitate too long once you arrive at the platform to rappell down, the Korean Marine instructor stationed there will push you off.

The school and the training were good and challenging. After completion of Mountain Warfare School, we had a battalion field meet with the Korean Marines. They roasted several pigs. These pigs were fat and juicy. When we smelled the aroma as they were roasting on the fire, our mouths were watering and we couldn't wait to feast upon them. We had several competitive events against the Korean Marines. One of them was a tug-of-war which we won. Though Korean Marines are smaller than most Marines, they are highly motivated, determined, and strong for their size. We even had some wrestling matches against them. You would be amazed at how they took some of the US Marines down, which clearly showed us that it doesn't matter how small one may be, but it is the determination and the fight in him.

Our last event was the relay race between the Korean Marines and our Company Commanders and the Battalion Commanders. Each Marine would run one lap around the track equivalent to the 400 meter run. The five Company Commanders of 2/5 ran in the following order: H&S, Weapons, Echo, Fox and Golf Company, and our Battalion Commander Lieutenant Colonel Kiley ran the last leg. Once the race started, the Korean Marines jumped out to a big lead. Echo Company Commander and my Company Commander, Captain Swindle, made up some distance, but it was not enough. By the time Lieutenant Colonel Kiley received the baton, the Korean Marine Colonel was flying and there was no way he was going to catch him. The battalion field meet was a great bonding between two allied forces that fought together side by side during the Korean War.

Our battalion had a few more training exercises that we conducted in South Korea. I was surprised that South Korean farmers with their families lived in the field where we trained. The ground was rock hard, so when we dug our fox holes, it took a little more time. While we were in the field, Marines keep up their hygiene. We packed shaving gear, soap, toothpaste, toothbrushes, wash cloths and towels, and each squad brought out several rolls of toilet paper. When we go to the bathroom, we find an isolated area and dig a hole with our E-Tool (entrenchment tool) and take a squat. When we came out of the field, a lot of Marines went to the hot tub houses in Pohang, which had these large tubs that could hold about 10-15 Marines. It was great to get a hot relaxing bath. When you got out, you would feel so refreshed.

When we went on liberty in Seoul, Korea, the Commander had chartered buses to take us there. It was an hour and a half drive from Camp Muchuk to Seoul, which is the Capital of South Korea, a very large city. Marines did a lot of shopping there like it was Christmas. You could get leather goods, mink coats, designer purses, clothes, and so much more for dirt cheap. We had bags and bags of goodies that we would send to loved ones, wives and girlfriends. After our two-month exercise training was completed in South Korea, our battalion flew back to Okinawa, Japan. When we arrived back in Japan, we spent the next few days cleaning our gear, weapons, washing our camouflaged fatigues, and getting fresh haircuts. The Japanese barbers on base could cut hair pretty good. You will always find a few Marines in the company that could cut hair, and make pretty good money on the side, besides their paycheck from Uncle Sam. After we squared all our gear away, we had a four-mile company run on Friday. After the run, we had a company formation. Captain Swindle briefed us that Golf Company along with the 81mm Mortar Section from Weapons Company will be flying out on Monday to Diego Garcia for 30 days. We would be cross-training with the British Royal Marines and standing guard duty.

We flew out of Kadena Air Force Base on Monday morning, and landed in the evening at the US Naval Base Diego Garcia. Once we arrived, we went through a Customs check, and after we finished, there were buses that took us to the area where we would be staying. The Island was beautiful, and there were US Navy personnel, both men and women who were stationed there that lived in co-ed barracks. When we arrived at our destination, each Platoon and the 81mm Mortar Section from Weapons

Company were given one-story barracks just big enough to hold a Platoon. They had double racks and wall lockers. We unpacked our sea bags, put our packs and H-harness on top of the wall lockers, and turned our weapons in to this small armory. We had a company formation, in which it was mandatory that the 81mm Mortar Section from Weapons Company stand at our formations too, since they were assigned to our Company under the command of Captain Swindle. We would start cross-training with the British Royal Marines the next day.

There was a Navy Petty Officer 1st Class, that gave us an overview of the base where everything was located, such as the PX which is a military store where you can purchase a variety of items such as clothes, shoes, colognes, radios, TV's and much more. He showed us the chow hall, snack bar, movie theatre, bike rental shops, and the bait and tackle shop which would provide everything you would need to go fishing. He also warned us if we went swimming in the ocean, to beware of sharks and jellyfish. There was a Navy male who had been recently stung by a jellyfish and was in serious condition.

After formation, 1st Sergeant Slate sounded liberty call. We were surprised that they cut us loose so early. Everyone went into the barracks and changed into civilian attire. Nine Marines from my Platoon including myself decided to rent bikes and explore the island. Riding around the island was beautiful. We hit the package store and everyone bought a case of beer. We rode down to the beach with a case of beer in one hand, and the other hand on the handlebar. When we arrived at the beach, there were some Navy females on the beach. We went over to them and introduced ourselves, and one of them jokingly said, "We know the Marines have landed, don't y'all come down here and tear our base up. We know how rowdy and destructive Marines are". We laughed and said we were going to be good boys, and try to be on our best behavior.

Sergeant Rodriguez Weapons Company 2/5 with local Islanders on U.S Naval Base Diego Garcia. Courtesy: Trent LaLand

Marines from Weapons Company 2/5 fishing and drinking beer on Diego Garcia. Courtesy: Trent LaLand

We stayed on the beach for about two hours, drinking and having fun. We then decided to go fishing, so we grabbed what beer we had left, jumped on our bikes and rode to the bait and tackle shop. If we could have gotten DUI's while riding bikes, we all would have had one. Our first day on Diego Garcia, we had a blast!

The next day we started cross-training with the British Royal Marines. They used black rubber Zodiac boats, which could hold about 8-10 Marines. We would be conducting day and night raid exercises at designated objectives on the island. On the day raids, the British Royal Marines would ride the Zodiac boats at full speed from the ocean onto the beach. We would dismount and attack an urban environment setting in company strength, clearing each building. At night, the raids were completely tactical. We would blacken our faces and paddle ashore from the ocean in black Zodiac boats. Then we would silently low-crawl to the objective using the night as the element of surprise to our advantage.

In addition to our Infantry Tactic Training Exercises, we still had Company and Platoon Physical Training. After thirty days in Diego Garcia, we flew back to Okinawa, Japan where we would complete the remainder of our training and 6-month deployment. The last week of our deployment, we cleaned and packed all our gear and flew back to the United States. My first deployment as a grunt was motivating, challenging and fun.

My first enlistment was for three years. In 1986, the Marine Corp was giving bonuses if you re-enlist as a 03 Infantry soldier. In June 1986, I re-enlisted for the bonus and received orders for Camp Lejeune, North

Carolina, 2nd Marine Division, 1st Battalion, 2nd Marines. You meet different Marines, leaders and Commanders, but nothing changes. No matter what Marine Infantry Battalion you were assigned to, the *Esprit de Corps* (which means our code of comrade) makes us elite and drives us.

I was assigned to Charlie Company 2nd Platoon. I went through the usual protocol where you meet the Company 1st Sergeant, the Platoon Commander, Platoon Sergeant, and your Squad Leader. My Platoon Sergeant, Staff Sergeant J. Cox, introduced me to the Platoon. I received a warm welcome from my new Platoon members. One by one, they introduced themselves by their name or nickname, saying welcome to 2nd Platoon. Lance Corporal Dennis Sanders and Lance Corporal Ronald Jackson said, *"Brother we're gonna take you under our wings, and when we're not training, we're gonna show you a good time, and where all the hot spots are. You're gonna love the Carolinas"*. When the weekend came, they took me out. Lance Corporal Sanders had a nice black and gray Mercury Cougar. The three of us left base on Friday evening heading down Hwy 17 south to Wilmington, North Carolina. It took us fifty minutes to get there. We got a room at a nice hotel, and after we got settled in, we went to Wrightsville Beach. It was a nice area with a lot of outdoor cafés and restaurants around the beach area. We stopped and ate at a restaurant that had live jazz on their outside balcony. When we were not in the field training, Lance Corporal Sanders, Lance Corporal Jackson and I would go out together the majority of the time. And on some occasions, we would link up with some of our fellow Marines from the Platoon. I started to get very familiar with North Carolina. Sometimes we would leave base early Saturday morning and head out to the University of North

Carolina in Chapel Hill. We also would travel to Charlotte, Raleigh, and others areas of North Carolina. Sometimes we would go to Myrtle Beach, South Carolina, and Norfolk, Virginia. We became friends with a lot of ladies, but none of us had made any commitments to any of them. We were just enjoying ourselves.

One Sunday, we decided to go to this popular park in Wilmington, North Carolina. It was there I met a young lady by the name of Janice. We hit it off pretty good. After a while, we started to spend some time together going out. We didn't make any commitments to one another, but we became real good friends. She was born and raised in Wilmington, North Carolina. She even knew NBA star Michael Jordan, where she went to Middle School and Laney High School with him.

My battalion became busy with more training exercises, so I was not able to spend as much time with her. I was promoted to Corporal and became a Fire Team Leader. We were scheduled for upcoming deployments to Okinawa, Japan and a six-month Mediterranean Float. After our six-month deployment, we were also scheduled to go through desert training and cold weather training. When we went to Okinawa, Japan, we conducted our jungle training at NTA. While going through the land navigation course, we went in fire teams, which were three men and one team leader. I had to do the map reconnaissance, plot the route using 6-8 digit grids, and getting the azimuths from one check point to the next. As you're doing this, you train the junior Marines on your team so they can understand and know what to do. You do not want to be a team leader and not know what you're doing.

This sets a bad example for the junior Marines under your leadership. Marine NCOs lead by example.

Desert Training was conducted at Twenty-nine Palms, California in the sweltering heat of the Mojave Desert, where temperatures in the daytime would go above 100 degrees, but amazingly, at night it gets 60 degrees and under. At night while sleeping in our foxholes, we would have to wrap up to stay warm. One morning while conducting a tactical company movement, there were at least 100 rattlesnakes in one area of the desert. I remember the Company 1st Sergeant saying, *"For you curious Marines, stay away from them, unless you want to get bitten and get real sick"*.

Cold Weather Training was conducted at Mountain Warfare Training Center in Bridgeport, California, in January 1990. By far, this was one of the most challenging training exercises that I went through as a Marine. The school trains Marines to maneuver on skis with full combat gear, and to fight in prolonged cold weather operations. Training takes place at the school at altitudes up to 8,500 feet and in temperatures below freezing. When we first arrived, we stayed down in the valley at the base camp. Right before we hiked up the mountain for approximately 25 days of training, we were hit by a blizzard. The Battalion Commander and Company Commanders received what they wanted, and that is for training to be close to reality as possible. It was about 0800 hrs when Charlie Company started up the mountain. Alpha Company went up one hour before us, and Bravo Company was coming up one hour behind us. As we were going up, it was tough because we were hiking into and against the blizzard wind. You could barely see 1st Platoon, who was in front of us, due to visibility. Everyone was wearing white parkas, white snow boots and white skis which were tied to our packs. We blended in with the snow. The majority of training was conducted on the Company level. After completion of Cold Weather Training, the battalion flew back to Camp LeJeune, North Carolina.

I have now been in the Marine Corp for seven years. I have trained in every climate, jungle, desert, and cold weather, as well as have crossed-trained with Foreign Military Units.

I was well diverse and knowledgeable in using other weapons of the Marine Corp. My favorite weapon that I carried, which all Team Leaders in the Infantry are assigned, is the M203 Grenade Launcher. I liked the M203 because of the dual firepower it had. Attached to the M16A2 rifle which fires a 5.56 round is a grenade launcher, which fires a 40 mm high-explosive grenade, as well as a buck shock round, CS GAS, smoke, and an illumination round. You have two sites on the M203 grenade launcher that you can use, which are the quadrant and leaf site. I preferred to use the leaf site, in which I could neatly drop a 40 mm grenade in the window of a building at a range of 300-400 meters. As Marines, we qualified on the rifle range with our personal weapons every year to ensure that we had the right elevation and windage on our weapons, or in other words, the right battle sight zero, in case we were called into combat. I have never been in a combat situation, but as Marines we are trained and prepared to respond at a moment's notice. At the present time, I did not know that the training I received in the Marines would be called into account later on in a real live situation.

In March 1990, Second Marines Regimental Guard needed a few Non-Commissioned Officers to be Corporal of the Guard (COG) and Sergeant of the Guard (SOG). I was one of the few NCO's chosen. I was the Senior Corporal and was designated the Sergeant of the Guard for one of the shifts. All I had to do was post and relieve Marine Sentry's standing guard duty on their post. I then would come back to the guard shack to monitor the radio. The Corporal of the Guard, Corporal Anthony Jones, would be in the guard shack with me. We took turns checking the area and the Marine guards on post. We would sit in the guard shack most of the time with our 9 mm pistols on our side, watching movies. We still ran physical training in the mornings to stay in shape. On my off time, I would go to Wilmington to spend quality time with Janice, who I was now dating. She wanted me to meet her family, which I did. I participated in a lot of her family gatherings, and would always get a home cooked meal at her Mother's house on the weekend. All of that came to an abrupt end when duty called.

Chapter 6

Deployed Operation Desert Shield

The first week of August 1990 on a Monday morning, we were having our regular morning formation. Staff Sergeant James Williams, who was our staff NCO, walked out and said *"Every Marine is to report to their unit immediately"*. We were all surprised, and I asked Staff Sergeant Williams *"What is the reason?"* He told me to just report back to my unit and they would tell me. The 2nd Marines Regimental Guard was a combination of Marines from 1st battalion 2nd Marines, 2nd battalion 2nd Marines, and 3rd battalion 2nd Marines. Corporal Jones and I were walking back to Charlie Company discussing what could possibly be going on. We arrived at the Company office, and the Company Gunnery Sergeant told us that there will be a Company formation at 1300 hrs, and that we would be assigned to the same Platoon. At 1300 hrs, I was standing tall in Formation with 2nd Platoon. The Company Commander came out to Formation with Platoon Commanders and the Company Executive Officer. The Company 1st Sergeant called the Company to attention, *"Charlie Company Ah-Ten-Hut"*. He then did an 'About Face' as the four Platoon Commanders took their positions in front of their Platoons. Every Platoon was full. My Platoon had 42 Marines and 1 Navy Corpsman standing tall. Included in that count were the Platoon Commander and Platoon Sergeant. Every Marine that had been on temporary assigned duty (TAD) had been recalled. The Company Commander sharply came in front of the

Company 1st Sergeant, standing at attention. 1st Sergeant Goodman renders a crisp salute sounding off *"Charlie Company, all present and accounted for"*. Captain Dysart returned the salute, and then 1st Sergeant Goodman took his position to the rear of the Company Commander. Captain Dysart gave the Company the command *"At ease"*. Everyone went to the modified position of parade rest. He then began to speak. *"Men you are all wondering why are we standing here? And why every Marine who was TAD has been recalled? I am about to solve your curiosity. The Iraqi Army has invaded Kuwait City, and 2nd Marine division has received marching orders to proceed to the area of Iraq. There are three scenarios that we are looking at. One, the Iraqi Army will withdraw from Kuwait before we arrive on station. Two, we arrive on station in the area of Iraq and begin a major build up of Military forces in preparation for an assault into Kuwait. Three, President Sadaam Hussein has no intentions of withdrawing his military forces from Kuwait, which gives us no choice but to assault Kuwait, physically removing the Iraqi Army by Military force thereby liberating Kuwait"*. Captain Dysart briefed us that we would be shipping out on Friday, which was only four days away. *"There are a lot of things that we need to accomplish in a very short time. The Navy ships will be coming down from Norfolk, Virginia to pick us up at the port in Morehead City, North Carolina. Our battalion will be an element of the 4th Marine Expeditionary Brigade. Alpha Company and Bravo Company will be embarked on board the USS Iwo Jima. Charlie Company will be the only Rifle Company embarked on board the USS Guam. Also our Battalion Commander Lieutenant Colonel Robert P. McAleer will be embarked on the Guam with us"*. Our Battalion was going on this deployment with a seasoned Battalion Commander. Lieutenant Colonel McAleer was commissioned as a 2nd Lieutenant on 3 June 1970 during the Vietnam War. He joined the Fleet Marine Force as a Rifle Platoon Commander in Bravo Company 1st Battalion 6th Marines. Captain Dysart then went on to say, *"There will be another Company formation at 1630 hrs. That is all for now. Platoon Commanders take charge of your Platoons"*. The four Platoon Commanders rendered salutes, and Captain Dysart returned their salute saying *"Carry out the plan of the day"*.

He then walked back to the company office. Every Marine was wondering, *"Where is Kuwait?"* My Platoon Commander, 2nd Lieutenant H.R. Vanopdorp had the Platoon form a horseshoe around him. He had a map with him and showed us where Kuwait was situated. It was a small neighboring city that was located outside of Iraq. He briefed us on what needed to take place before the 1630 hrs formation, as well as the agenda for the rest of the week before we shipped out on Friday. We marched over to Supply to get our desert-camouflaged fatigues, two-quart canteens, and other accessories. After that, we began to pack our gear, and for the Marines and Navy personnel who were not married and who had personal owned vehicles (POVs) and motorcycles, there were designated storage areas on Marine Corps Base Camp Lejeune (North Carolina) where we would store them on Thursday.

Everyone was making phone calls to family members and making out last will and testaments, just in case we were killed in combat or died while serving overseas. Each service member had the SGLI (Service members Group Life Insurance), being automatically insured for the maximum amount of $150,000. In the last will and testament, we could designate who the beneficiary or beneficiaries were that would receive the SGLI, as well as any funds in our bank accounts and any valuables such as cars, motorcycles, TVs, stereo equipment, etc. The last will and testament would be signed by the Marine and military legal officer, and notarized in the presence of a witness. The documents would eliminate any dispute between family members.

I called my parents and explained to them what was going on and that I would be shipping out on Friday. My mother got a little emotional, and I told her not to worry because I would be okay. She said she knew I would because God is going to watch over me and protect me. I then talked to my father, who had served in the Korean War. He said *"I'll see you when you get home Son. You're gonna be okay"*. I replied *"Roger that Dad"*.

After I talked to my parents, I called Janice and told her. She was shocked and said *"I can't believe it....just like that, you're shipping out on Friday"*. I told her that sometimes it happens like that. She asked if she would be able to see me before I left, and I told her *"Of course!"* We spent two evenings together (Wednesday and Thursday). On Wednesday evening, we went out to dinner at Red Lobster in Jacksonville, NC, which is the city located right outside of the base. The day before we were to ship out (Thursday), our authorized free time or liberty was restricted to the Marine Corps Base only. So Janice drove down to MCB Camp Lejeune from Wilmington, NC to spend the last day with me. We spent some quality quiet time together. On Friday morning, reveille was at 0400 hrs. We marched over to the Chow Hall by Platoons and ate breakfast at 0430 hrs. After we ate, we marched over to the Armory to draw our weapons and night-vision devices. The chartered buses that would take us to Morehead City, NC, arrived at 0630 hrs.

We had a company formation with all of our gear at 0700 hrs to board the buses. Right before formation, the Marines and Navy personnel who had family members there said their goodbyes. They were kissing their wives and children, and there was a lot of crying. They all thought *"Will this be the last time I see my loved ones?"*

The Company 1st Sergeant walked up and said *"Hurry up and get those last kisses in, because if you're going where the action is, it's this way. Fall into formation, Marines"*. When all four Platoons had fallen into formation, the Company 1st Sergeant called the Company to attention.

	Charlie Company Ah-Ten-Hut, Right Face, Forward March
	Ah-Left, Right-Left, Ah-Left-Right-Left
	(1st Sergeant sang cadence while the families watched us march to the buses.)
	I used to date a Beauty Queen (then the company would repeat his cadence)
	Now I'm hiking an M16
1st Sgt	*I used to drive a Cadillac....Now I'm hiking a combat pack*
Company	*I used to drive a Cadillac....Now I'm hiking a combat pack*
	Delay Cadence, Delay Cadence, Delay Cadence Count
Company	*1 . . .*
1st Sgt	*Can't Hear You*

Company	*2 . . .*
1st Sgt	***A Little Louder Now***
Company	*3 . . .*
1st Sgt	***Sound- in Good Now***
Company	*4 . . .*
1st Sgt	***Take It Home Now***
Company	*1 – 2 – 3 – 4*
Company Cadence Speed	

> ***1 – 2 – 3 – 4 United States Marine Corps,***
> ***OORAH***

1st Sgt gives the Command

> ***Company HALT!***

We then boarded the buses. As we were driving away, family and friends were standing in the parking lot crying, waving American and yellow flags and saying *"We love you"*. With flashing lights on their cruisers, the Marine Military Police blocked the roads to stop traffic so that the convoy of buses could get through the busy streets. All along our route to Morehead City, NC, people were on the sides of the road waving flags and signs that said ***"GOD BLESS OUR TROOPS", "GOOD LUCK", and "WE ARE PRAYING FOR YOU"***. It meant a lot to us to see how much people truly cared about us and how they actually showed their support.

When we arrived at the Port of Morehead City, NC, our Company Gunnery Sergeant who was part of the advanced party was there to meet us (Charlie Company) and show us where our sleeping quarters would be while on board the USS Guam. Alpha and Bravo Companies boarded the USS Iwo Jima. The majority of the Marines had been on ships before, either in training exercises or six-month deployments. So being embarked on a Navy ship was nothing new to us. We settled in pretty quickly, and at 1500 hrs the Amphibious Task Force (ATF) was underway. It would take us over two weeks to arrive on station in the area of Iraq.

My Squad Leader, Sergeant J.B. Jennings, just rejoined our Platoon the day we embarked on board the USS Guam. He had just completed US Army Ranger School at Fort Benning, Georgia. Marines received quotas to go through schools of other US branches of service. Army Ranger School is one of the school's that is highly requested by Marines. Sergeant Jennings had lost a lot of weight going through Ranger School. Some of the members of our Platoon teased him about how he looked pale as a ghost. With physical training on the schedule, it would be just a matter of time before he would regain his weight and color back.

As we proceeded to our destination, everyday was approached as a normal workday, except Sunday when we were scheduled off. The sleeping quarters on the ship are called berthing areas, which can be very tight spaces. The beds are like bunk beds, except there are four in a row. There would be four Marines to each bunk bed, and there is a slot on each bed where you would lock up your rifles. We would place our h-harness, helmets and packs with gear inside them on the outer ends of the bed. We also had one wall locker for personal gear such as hygiene items. Our sea bags and night-vision devices for each Platoon were stored in a designated section of the berthing area.

All of our commanders stayed in the officer's quarters which were located in a different area of the ship, and the staff NCOs' sleeping quarters were also located in a designated area of the ship. Every morning, we either ran Company or Platoon PT (physical training) on the flight deck of the ship. The majority of the time, we had Platoon PT. When we ran, we would be in full gear: boots, utilities, rifle and pack. My Platoon Commander, 2nd Lieutenant Vanopdorp, was tall and slim. And when he ran, he would step it out with his long legs and push the Platoon hard. He was going to make sure we were in excellent shape. As the days passed, the ATF eventually arrived on station in the area of Iraq. Word came down the chain of command that President Saddam Hussein had no intentions of withdrawing the Iraq Army from Kuwait.

The U.S. Forces and Allies would begin a major buildup of forces, weapons and equipment to begin training operations in preparation for an assault into Kuwait City. This would be the largest buildup of U.S. military forces since the Vietnam War. While on station in the North Arabian Sea in preparation for the war, we were told what our command structure consisted of. U.S. Navy Vice Admiral Henry H. Mauz, Jr. was Commander of the Naval Component of U.S. Central Command (NAVCENT). Rear Admiral John B. "Bat" LaPlante commanded the amphibious element, which consisted of 31 US Navy ships loaded with two Marine expeditionary brigades (MEB), and one special operations capable Marine expeditionary unit (MEU SOC) which consisted of roughly 17,000 Marines. Not since Operation Steel Pike in 1964 has there been this big of a buildup of US Naval Amphibious Forces. Rear Admiral LaPlante's counterpart was Marine Major General Harry W. Jenkins Jr., who commanded both the 4th Marine Expeditionary Brigade and as the most senior Marine officer afloat, also commanded the overall Marine landing force, including the 5th Marine Expeditionary Brigade and

13th Marine Expeditionary Unit Special Operations Capable.

Amphibious Squadron 6 was commanded by Navy Captain Alan B. Moser, who was among the first of the naval forces to sail to the Arabian Sea after Iraq's invasion of Kuwait. Captain Moser's squadron consisted of five ships loaded with around 2,100 Marines from units of Major General Jenkins 4th MEB. The 4th MEB would begin training in the Desert of Oman, a neighboring country of Saudi Arabia. Our training exercises would have the code name "Sea Soldier 1" through however many training operations that would be conducted before the start of the war. The training operations were code named "Sea Soldier" because we were elite soldiers that would come from the sea. We began to have classes about the Iraq Army, studying their tactics, their special unit (the Republican Guard), and their weapons. Our first training exercise in the Desert of Oman would last 10 days. This would become the normal routine for each "Sea Soldier" exercise. We would train for 10 days in the desert, and then we would have 3-4 days downtime on the ship, and then back to the desert for another 10 days of training.

The first exercise Charlie Company conducted was a helo-bourne assault in a designated location in the Desert of Oman. We touched down about 12 noon. Training in the Desert of Oman was like any other desert – scorching hot, dry, humid with no shade, no trees, and with temperatures reaching 110-115 degrees. The company moved in a tactical formation from 12 noon until 0300 hrs. We moved for 15 straight hours with just four breaks. When we finally stopped, everyone was dead-tired, and the temperature had dropped tremendously. The company set up into a 360-degree perimeter for the remainder of the night. Charlie Company also took part in Operation Imminent Thunder, which was conducted in Saudi Arabia (25 miles south of the Kuwaiti border).

During that operation, Charlie Company linked up with 1st Marine expeditionary force Task Force Ripper based in the Desert of Saudi Arabia. The 1st Battalion 7th Marines, who were based there, were able to give Charlie Company a tour of a mock Iraqi strong point, as well as pass on valuable lessons learned. We had been at sea and training in the desert close to 90 days, without any liberty ports and without any phone calls. Everyone would look forward to mail call. That is when we would receive letters and care packages from friends, family members, girlfriends, wives, churches, and different schools (middle schools to colleges). When I received mail from Janice, I would just melt into her letters and words. Receiving mail while you are deployed overseas is a big morale booster. But I have seen Marines become discouraged when the Platoon Sergeant who passes out the mail does not call their name, when they are looking forward to receiving mail from family members (especially from wives).

There was a Marine in my Platoon named Corporal George Hammond who was married and did not receive mail from his wife for three straight mail calls. He started telling me *"Man, she's cheating on me, I know she is"*. I tried to encourage Corporal Hammond and tell him that maybe we would have the opportunity to make phone calls soon, and then he could talk to his wife. That opportunity became a reality not long after our conversation.

After being at sea for over 98 straight days with no phone calls and no liberty ports, the commanders decided it was time to get us a liberty port. We landed a liberty port call in an Arabic country called Dubai.

U.S.S. GUAM in port at Dubai. Courtesy: Trent LaLand

We were all looking forward to drinking a few cold frosty beers. The Company 1st Sergeant was asking for volunteers to be guests at the homes of wealthy Arabians who would be serving as hosts as a gesture of friendship to US soldiers. I decided to volunteer. On 24 November 1990, we pulled into port at Dubai. There were ten Marines in the group I was with that would be going to one of the Arabian houses to be their guests. When we arrived at our Arabian host's house, it was very nice and laid-out with state-of-the-art furniture. He had these sweet pastries prepared for us that he wanted us to eat. When we started eating them, we found them to be extremely too sweet. After eating only a few, he insisted we eat more. We obliged and gulped them down so as not to offend him.

After we finished our fellowship with our Arabian host, we said our goodbyes and left to find a place where we could sit down, relax and drink a cold beer. We found a location that had a large lounge area, indoor swimming pool, and a bowling alley. There were a lot of Marines and Sailors already there. My fellow Platoon member and good friend, Corporal David Jenkins, was with me. We ordered two beers and sat down. That first cold frosty beer was so good and smoothly went down the whistle. Corporal Jenkins and I walked over to the swimming pool balcony. There were about a dozen Marines leaning over the balcony. In the swimming pool were two beautiful Arabian women in bathing suits talking. They noticed we were gazing at them. One of them started going off and yelling, *"What are you looking at?"* We didn't say a word. We all just walked away so that we wouldn't cause an altercation. The only women we had seen in the last three months were the ones in our dreams. After being at sea for 98 straight days, this port call was much needed because when you are embarked on a Navy ship that is filled with Marines and Sailors for a long period of time, stress levels and tensions can rise. We stayed in Dubai from 24 November to 4 December. And on 5 December 1990, we pulled out to sea to prepare for our next training exercise. We were also told that Vice Admiral Stanley R. Arthur assumed command of NAVCENT.

On 8 December 1990, it was late at night when suddenly Corporal Dennis Betz from the Company's Weapons Platoon took sick and became gravely ill. The Navy Corpsman from that Platoon was able to get him up to the ship's sick bay. We learned later the next day that a blood vessel in his brain had ruptured and that the ship's surgeon had performed surgery to release pressure on his brain. On 9 December 1990, we were preparing to go back in the Desert of Oman the next day for Sea Soldier III training exercise when we received the sad news that Corporal Dennis Betz had passed away. He was a hard-working dedicated Marine. His body was flown off ship by helicopter to a location where his remains would be transported by a military C-130 cargo plane to Dover Air Force Base in Delaware.

On 10 December 1990 while our company was in the Desert of Oman for Sea Soldier III, we had a memorial service for Corporal Dennis Betz that was conducted by the Battalion Chaplain. It was only one month before that Corporal Stephen, Corporal Jenkins and I from our Platoon, along with Corporal Trudell from 3rd Platoon and Corporal Dennis Betz, went up before a board made up of staff non-commissioned officers from Charlie Company. This was called a Meritorious Sergeant Board, which is when Corporals from the Company are excelling and are chosen to compete against each other to be upgraded to the rank of Sergeant. And now, just like that, Corporal Dennis Betz was gone.

It hit me like a ton of bricks. There was no guarantee that none of us would make it home from this deployment as we prepared for the war with Iraq. He was married and had two kids. Thoughts came to my mind that there would be Marines in uniform and a Chaplain knocking at the door of his home at Camp LeJeune, North Carolina to tell his wife the sad news. Then she would have to comfort their two young children and tell them that their Daddy would not be coming home. Corporal Dennis Betz will be sadly missed by all of us. This really made me think. I just wanted to draw closer to God, so I began to pray more frequently. Afterwards, we continued moving forward training and preparing for the war. No one knew when the war would start. But our commanders were making sure we would be ready when it did. On 18 December 1990, the helicopters picked us up in the Oman Desert and flew us back to the ship. Sea Soldier III would be our last training exercise for the year. When we arrived back on the GUAM, we cleaned all the sand off of our gear and washed down everything. For the Marines who had serious cases of sunburn and cracked lips, the down time would allow the affected areas to heal. While on ship when we were not training, the Navy was good at providing activities to keep the morale up for Marines and Sailors while at sea. The biggest event was the steel beach picnic (a tradition in the United States Navy), which is a department sponsored barbecue held on the flight deck of the ship. After 45 consecutive days at sea, Marines and Sailors are authorized to have two beers which we would receive when the ship scheduled the steel beach picnic. During the picnic, we would have grilled steaks, hamburgers, hot dogs, and a delicious spread that the Marine and Navy cooks provided.

There was a variety of activities and contests going on. There were two official GUAM talent shows, a basketball tournament, tattoo contest, Frisbee toss, live music and casino night on the mess decks. Besides the steel beach picnic, other activities that the GUAM would host were Weekend Bingo, Crazy Hat, T-shirt, Sneaker day contest and Galactic Grub Night where the cooks made Galactic Burgers so thick that you couldn't even get your mouth around it. In addition to the ship's activities for morale boosters, Charlie Company would have board games and spade tournaments in our sleeping quarters. My friend Corporal David Jenkins and I entered the spades tournament as teammates. Each team put twenty-five dollars in the pot. And when it was all said and done, we won the tournament and took the pot of money which was two hundred fifty dollars that we split. We also did a boot camp skit where I played the Senior Drill Instructor, and we videotaped it. When we completed it, we played it so the rest of the Company could watch it. The video was hilarious! During the night, we would spend time watching movies, writing letters and reading books. And there was a lot of pornographic reading material floating around the sleeping quarters. Sometimes at night while the ship was anchored in the middle of the ocean, me and a few other Marines would go sit on the flight deck of the GUAM, relaxing and talking. It was a beautiful view and very peaceful. The ocean was calm, the wind was gently blowing, and the moon was full and bright.

One of the most valuable lessons that I learned while on deployment overseas as a small unit leader, and especially during a wartime situation where your deployment can be long, hard and grueling, is that you must be able to encourage and motivate your men in extremely stressful environments and circumstances. A leader must not show any signs of weakness or breakdowns. A leader must know his men's weak points and strong points. Some Marines may not show any warning signs of deep depression or suicidal tendencies. A leader must be able to identify any behavioral changes in his men, talk to them regularly as a group and one-on-one. If they are not receiving mail from their family or wives, a leader must be wise and creative in strengthening and boosting up their morale. It is also good to encourage your Marines to attend church services on board ship. Some Marines who normally do not attend any church go to the ship's services to draw closer to God, to find inner peace from Him, and also to make peace with God just in case they don't make it back.

On 22 December 1990, we pulled into the Port of Muscat Oman (which is the capital of Oman) for our second liberty call that would last for 4 days. Already in port was the US Navy hospital ship the USNS Mercy, which we all knew was loaded with female nurses. Liberty call was sounded at 1300 hrs for the embarked Marines and Sailors. Corporal David Jenkins and I changed into our civilian clothes and made our way into town. We found a Burger King and ate there; but it definitely did not taste like the Burger Kings in the states. After we ate, we found the place where all the nurses from USNS Mercy were lounging. The place was like a USO Club: there was food, alcohol and phones to make calls back home. There was a deejay that played a combination of R&B, rock-n-roll, country and even some Motown music from the 60s. The majority of my Platoon was there. Corporal Jenkins and I asked two nurses to dance with us, and they did. After the song was over, we invited them to sit down with us, and they gladly accepted the invitation. We ordered some drinks and drank casually. We got to know each other and had a really good conversation. Today would be their last day in port because they were pulling out in the morning. We stayed together the rest of the evening talking and dancing. We exchanged addresses to write each other just as friends during the deployment. It was getting close to our curfew to be back on the GUAM which was 2300 hrs. Right before we were getting ready to leave, the deejay played *"Stand By Me"* by Ben E. King. We danced that last dance with them. And after the dance, they wished us good luck, hugged us and we said our goodbyes.

25 December 1990, Christmas Day, would be our last day in port. It was good to be able to make phone calls home and wish everyone a Merry Christmas. The Navy and Marine cooks prepared a delicious Christmas dinner, and we received a lot of mail and care packages from family, church groups, and schools. We pulled out of port on the morning of 26 December 1990. Back at sea again and as the days went by, everyone was wondering when the assault on Kuwait would begin – we were ready to go. 1 January came quickly. We were now in the New Year 1991. We had been at sea since August 1990. We had a church service on 1 January, and the Navy and Marine cooks prepared another fine meal. The ship hosted Bingo for the embarked Marines and Sailors later that evening. It was just another day at sea, but that would quickly change on 1 January 1991.

This Portion Of The Cruisebook Is Dedicated
To The Memory Of:

Cpl Dennis William Betz
Wpns Plt, "C" Co, 1st Bn, 2nd Mar

Born: 7 Jul 1968   Enlisted: 18 Feb 1986   Died: 9 Dec 1990

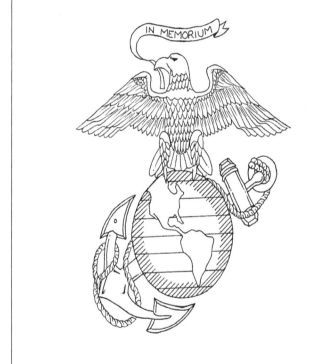

131

Chapter 7

Night Mission to Mogadishu

As Rear Admiral John B. "Bat" LaPlante increased the tempo of war preparation, NAVCENT received an alert message indicating that civil war and internal clan conflict in Somalia, Africa might endanger US citizens, and therefore required a military response. This warning did not surprise Vice Admiral Stanley R. Arthur, Commander of NAVCENT, who had been monitoring message traffic from Somalia and had noticed it as an increasing sense of urgency. The conditions on the ground in Mogadishu, Somalia had become critical. US Ambassador to Somali, James K. Bishop, realized that Somalia President Siad Barre had lost his grip of power in Somalia.

Since 1989, two major resistance organizations had taken up arms in Somalia against the regime of Siad Barre. President Siad Barre, who was nicknamed the "Earth Scorcher" by rebels, had taken power in 1969 and ruled the country with a stern hand since that time. Armed resistance had been picking up against the Siad Barre regime in the late 1980s. In late 1990, there were three main rebel organizations active in Somalia: the Somali National Movement (SNM); the Somali Patriotic Movement (SPM); and the United Somali Congress (USC). The SPM had taken up arms against the government in 1989, and the USC in July 1990. The increasing rebel activity led the regime to adopt reforms. The rebels dismissed these reforms as meaningless and called for an end to Siad Barre's control of the country.

Major Somali Rebel Movements, December 1990

Somali National Movement (SNM)	**Active in northern Somalia Oldest Movement (formed in London in early 1980s)**
Somali Patriotic Movement (SPM)	**Operational in southern Somalia Largely from Ogaden Started fighting in mid-1989**
United Somali Congress (USC)	**Active in central Somalia Primarily from Hawiye tribe Formed in 1989, commenced fighting in mid-1990**

In October 1990, the SNM stepped up its attacks on government forces and the USC began an offensive from its bases in Central Somalia, which quickly gained success against the government forces. By late November, signs of disintegration in the government were readily apparent from the disappearance of government daily newspapers from the newsstands, due to a paper shortage to increased banditry inside Mogadishu. By the beginning of December, USC rebel forces led by General Mohamed Farrah Aidid were reported to be within 30 miles of Mogadishu.

Mohamed Farrah Aidid was born in the Mudug region of Somalia. He was educated in Rome and Moscow, and served in the Italian colonial police force in the 1950s. Later he rose in the military of President Siad Barre to the rank of general and served in the 1977-78 Ogaden War with Ethiopia. Aidid also served in President Siad Barre's cabinet and as Somali ambassador to India before finally being appointed intelligence chief. In 1979, President Siad Barre suspected General Aidid of planning a coup and had him imprisoned for six years as means of pre-emption. Now Mohamed Farrah Aidid, who once served under President Siad Barre and imprisoned by him, is successfully advancing his rebel forces against Siad Barre's military forces. Aidid USC forces armaments included twin-barrel anti-aircraft guns mounted on trucks, light and heavy mortars, Browning machine-guns, and a wide variety of assault rifles. The government reacted with offers of mediation, and peace negotiations between the government and the rebel movements were scheduled for 11 through 13 December 1990 in Cairo. This fell through, however, because none of the three major movements were willing to participate. An SNM radio commentator phrased it this way: *"This last distress call by Siad Barre can fool no one. The dictatorial regime's tenure has reached its end, and no amount of dishonest diplomacy can save it. Let us hasten to overthrow the dictatorial regime and throw it into the trash".*

The Somalia state was in the final stages of complete state collapse. In mid-December 1990, President Siad Barre declared a state of emergency as USC and SNM rebel forces advanced toward Mogadishu. Civil war had reached the Somali capital of Mogadishu much faster than anyone had predicted. Trapped in the middle of

Somalia's bloody civil war were American nationals, private citizens, foreign diplomats and civilians. The civil war in Somalia was described as a war of all against all. Threats to foreigners escalated tremendously, and there was little regard for civilians or diplomatic privilege.

James K. Bishop was sworn in as US Ambassador to the Democratic Republic of Somalia in July 1990. Violence had been endemic in Mogadishu for many months. During the summer, embassies and government buildings had been bombed by the regime's opponents, and senior police officials had been assassinated. Westerners, including one of the US Embassy Marines, had been injured in a robbery and others had been killed in criminal attacks. US Ambassador James K. Bishop and his family had encountered this violence soon after their arrival when a shot was fired at his wife by a gang of thieves during a robbery at a supposedly safe beach. The violence was as much, or more, crime-related as part of the civil war. The US Embassy had earlier withdrawn all American personnel to the part of Mogadishu where the Chancery and other Embassy buildings were located on a 160-acre compound. Self-imposed travel restrictions and a curfew were intended to keep official Americans, foreigners and diplomats out of harm's way. The four-wheel drive vehicles used by international organizations were favorite gang targets; drivers were apt to be killed for their vehicles. In December, the self-imposed travel restrictions and curfew were proving to be inadequate as criminal activity grew. Vehicles were being taken and their drivers killed by soldiers, policemen, rebels and common criminals throughout the city and at all hours of the day.

A robbery and gunfight outside the Chancery Compound in early December made it evident that distance from the centers of earlier violence no longer provided any real protection. For several months, there had been frank discussions of the security situation at the community meetings open to both official and private Americans. Everyone familiar with the US Embassy knew that the top priority now was to take measures that would improve the physical security of Americans and the ability to cope with emergencies. Few Americans therefore seemed surprised when at a standing-room-only special community meeting 5 December 1990, US Ambassador James K. Bishop told everyone that he was recommending a voluntary departure of US government dependents and non-essential employees to Washington (which included his wife and daughter among the early evacuees). Subsequent telephone calls to parents and children at post emphasized the desirability of the children's early departure. Most foreign missions in Mogadishu took similar actions, and the United Nations (UN) was evacuating almost all of its 300 employees as the fighting increased and social disintegration worsened.

Well before those leaving voluntarily had flown off, Ambassador Bishop and his staff had recognized several of the benchmarks they had set to identify the time when ordered departure for US government employees should begin. The tide of violence was swelling. Another US Embassy driver, the second in three weeks, was shot and his vehicle stolen. The daily light-arms fire around the Embassy took an ominous turn when a firefight on the road outside the Embassy's Gate 1 sent bullets flying through the air and into the Vice-Consul's home on the US Compound, just as Embassy employees left for the day.

By 19 December 1990, the official American community had been reduced from 147 to 37 people, and the majority of the private Americans in Somalia were thought to have left as well. Between 19 and 30 December 1990, Ambassador Bishop and his staff were busy packing up the belongings of those who had departed, rehearsing their emergency procedures and trying to encourage both cabinet members and opposition leaders to curb the violent activities of their followers. But the situation only became more acute as an eruption of intertribal fighting in the capital added to the lawlessness. In the closing days of December, US Ambassador James K. Bishop met with Somali President Siad Barre and his Prime Minister and talked with him about what he saw as the future. This was after his military forces had come back into Mogadishu, after having been trounced in a battle outside the capital. President Barre told Ambassador Bishop that it was in the hands of God. After the meeting, Ambassador Bishop concluded that the government had neither a plan nor the ability to control the growing crisis. He could see the defeat in President Siad Barre's eyes.

As carnage and lawlessness spread, the need to evacuate remaining Americans increased while the ability to do so decreased. Ambassador Bishop's plans to further reduce their numbers were overtaken by the 30 December 1990 uprising. On that day, Mogadishu erupted in fighting with government forces, using all weaponry on hand in an attempt to crush the growing USC presence in the capital. Its nature and extent were not yet clear, but the firing which broke out throughout much of the city made it evident that the Americans still there were dealing with violence on a new order of magnitude. The greater danger was personalized the next morning when the Embassy's defense attaché, Colonel Ken Culwell, arrived at the Compound with several bullet holes in his car. One shell had found a gap in the vehicle's armor and cut across the driver's seat an inch behind Culwell's backbone. A bullet hole in the roof of another defense attaché office vehicle parked beside the Chancery reminded US Embassy personnel of the damage that stray rounds flying into the Compound could do to less resistant surfaces. That evening, the deputy OMC Chief Lieutenant Colonel Neil Youngman was attacked at an impromptu road block by an impatient Somali government soldier. The soldier sprayed the deputy chief's vehicle with bullets from his AK-47 assault rifle. Luckily, the deputy chief managed to escape. He was able to drive the vehicle back to the US Compound on the rims of the tires, thankful that only the front tires had received fatal punctures.

From 30 to 31 December 1990, Ambassador Bishop moved almost everyone into relatively secure areas, in and around the US Embassy and the K-7 Compound across Afgoy Road. Ambassador Bishop had hoped that the US Embassy staff could sit out the fighting behind the Compound walls. However, the insurgents would not negotiate or be cowed. They held their own in the eastern neighborhoods and attacked government strongholds at the Presidential Compound and the airport. From a US Embassy rooftop, as tracer fire lit up the skies over Somalia on New Year's Eve 1990, Karen Aguilar and some foreign-service friends broke into a bittersweet chorus of "Amazing Grace". Then someone opened fire on the astonished diplomats, and they ran for cover. Directly in front of them, they could see a 50 caliber machine-gun round that drilled into a garden right where they stood. A frightened Karen Aguilar told her friends that, *"We are not going to be able to save ourselves. Either we are going to get blown away or somebody is going to have to save us".*

The next day, New Year's Day, 1 January 1991, had proved to be Ambassador Bishop's last early morning jog around the Chancery Compound. His jog was aborted when small arms fire around the Embassy forced him to take cover three times in 20 minutes. Nervous soldiers made Afgoy Road a shooting gallery that same morning, cutting off from the Embassy those safe-havened outside its walls. The US Embassy began to open their gate to send armored vehicles to pick up people or to receive evacuees, only when lookouts posted on the roof of the K-7 apartment building radioed that no armed personnel were on the road. Communicator Matt Kula, Administrative Counselor Chris Swenson and Buildings Maintenance Officer Bill Mueller's sunburned faces became their lookout badges of office. Among the thousands of Somalis who began streaming past the US Embassy gate on their way out of the embattled city were members of the families of the embassies' Somali employees. Many of the latter, as well as numerous contract guards, were staying on the US Compound overnight because their homes were beyond government lines. The New Year brought the first request from the remaining private Americans seeking refuge within the US Compound. US A.I.D. Director Mike Rugh took on the task of housing and maintaining order for a Compound population that ultimately exceeded 500. US A.I.D. Contractor Peggy O'Rourke, the Embassy Irish-Jewish mother who had been preparing meals for 50 foreign service nationals and guards at the now vacated A.I.D. Compound, took over the Embassy Snack Bar Kitchen. While there, she was ultimately to prepare hot meals for some 350 evacuees, FSNs, and guards.

Ambassador Bishop's executive assistant, Lynda Walker, Nurse Practitioner Karen McGuire Rugh, and PAO Karen Aguilar took over direction of the Embassy kitchens, and began providing gourmet cooking for the Embassy staff. By 2 January 1991, the government was employing heavy artillery against rebel forces whose strength nevertheless appeared to be increasing. Italian officials made a fruitless effort to arrange a cease fire among the factions. With the failure of this effort, the American ambassador realized his options were narrowing, and on 2 January 1991, he made the frantic call to Washington D.C. stating that they would need US military assistance in departing a city in which the lives of Americans were now seriously endangered. His message was clear and frank: *"If a US Military Rescue Force does not arrive in time, there will be no one to rescue"*. His urgent request for help received immediate attention in Washington D.C., and set in motion the planning and execution of Operation Eastern Exit, which came to be considered by many a model for this type of action.

The Pentagon moved quickly in response to Ambassador Bishop's 2 January 1991 request for military assistance; the execute order was issued before the end of the day. The Chairman of the Joint Chiefs of Staff (CJCS) execute order directed USCINCCENT to: (a) deploy 2 C-130s and 1 AC-130 plus security team; (b) deploy LPH, LPD and appropriate escort at best speed consistent with preparations for extraction and weather to MODLOC vicinity Mogadishu. Conduct helicopter extraction of American citizens (AMCITS) at American Embassy (AMEMBASSY) Mogadishu as soon as possible while optimizing survivability of extraction forces; and (c) provide Operational Order (OPORD) as soon as possible: advise earliest possible time for commencement of extraction operations.

The Secretary of Defense (SECDEF) execution order noted that armed helicopter escort and armed security contingent on extraction helicopters (or on C-130's if used) was authorized. Various possibilities had been under consideration at all levels of command from the beginning of the crisis, and it had not yet become clear that only one option remained viable. The preferred course of action involved sending aircraft with security detachments on board into the Mogadishu airport and flying American evacuees out of the country. Several other foreign missions had done exactly that during the last few days of December. Central Command also considered the use of special operation forces, going so far as to direct that six MH-53 pave low helicopters with tanker support be prepared to conduct the mission. This option never progressed beyond the initial concept, because the pave low helicopters were preparing for the imminent launching of Desert Storm. Additionally, the special operations forces were heavily committed along the Iraqi border and in the western desert looking for scud missiles.

CINCCENT Eastern Exit Force Options

Organization	Task
1. CENTAF	Stage three C-130s and one AC-130 in preparation for evacuation in a permissive environment. ARCENT deployed one MP security Platoon to provide security of the NEO force at Mogadishu airport
2. NAVCENT	Deploy designated naval forces at best speed of advance (SOA) to Station off Mogadishu to conduct NEO while optimizing survivability of extraction forces. Low intensity resistance should be expected
3. SOCCENT	Be prepared to deploy six MH-53s and appropriate tanker support tanker to conduct NEO of American Embassy, Mogadishu

Later in the day, Ambassador Bishop was told that the President of the United States had ordered C-130s to fly immediately to Nairobi, Kenya. They would be prepared to fly into Mogadishu as soon as flight clearances could be obtained and arrangements made for Americans to proceed safely to the airport. In addition, US Naval forces had been ordered to set course for Mogadishu from their positions in the Gulf of Oman. By 7 January 1991, they would be able to evacuate the Americans by helicopters from the US Embassy itself if it became necessary.

Although Mogadishu's phones were out, the US Embassy was able to communicate with most Western European embassies by radio.

The US Embassy's efforts to obtain landing clearance for the US Air Force C-130s at Mogadishu airport were frustrated by their inability to communicate with anyone in the government. The Embassy sent a runner to the foreign ministry office, who found its gates chained and the building vacant. The Embassy then contacted the Italians who informed them that they had communicated with President Siad Barre, who had agreed in principle that foreign governments could evacuate their nationals. He told the Italians that details were to be worked out with the foreign ministry office, but the foreign ministry gates were chained and the building was vacant. It was obvious that command and control within government forces was eroding fast. The US Embassy began receiving reports that government soldiers had shot officers when given orders to, which they objected. Ambassador Bishop's main concern was the protection of Americans. Conditions at Mogadishu airport were uncertain, and there was absolutely no communication with the airport because all telephone lines were down. More importantly, the airport was nearly two miles from the US Embassy, and Ambassador Bishop did not believe Americans could travel safely through the embattled city. It now became apparent that their only hope to be rescued would have to come from US Naval expeditionary forces from the sea.

On 3 January 1991, Ambassador Bishop advised Washington that the C-130 option was impractical, and evacuation by ship-based helicopters from the Amphibious

Task Force remains the only option and hope for survival. The warning and execution order was received on board the flagship USS Nassau (LHA 4), which was then on the last day of a port call in Dubai, UAE. Upon receipt of the order in the ship's tactical command center, the duty officer immediately took the order to Vice Admiral Stanley Arthur, Commander of NAVCENT, who read the order. PHIBGRU TWO (PG-2) was given a one-hour deadline for a proposal for an amphibious force to execute Eastern Exit. CPG-2 looked at the closest amphibious ships to Mogadishu, those off the coast of Oman, to be the components of the contingency Amphibious Task Force (ATF). Two LPHs, an LPD and LSD, and three LSTs were in the anchorage at that time. Also present were two MPS ships and five replenishment ships. BB-63 Missouri was nearby with three escorts.

Table 5.   PHIBGRU TWO Proposed Amphibious
Task Force Capabilities

LPD   *Trenton* had a CH-53E detachment aboard, thus
      providing a heavy lift and long-range helicopter
      option. Embarked troops included Navy SEALs
      and   BSSG-4   personnel   (including   Military
      Police).

LPH   *Guam* had two squadrons of CH-46s embarked
      as well as BLT 1/2, thus providing a mass troop
      lifts capability. Also embarked were a large
      medical   contingent   from   BSSG-4   and   the
      alternative command group of FOURTH MEB
      (FOURTH MEB DET ONE).

LSD   *Pensacola* had three LCACs aboard the LAVs,
      which   would   provide   an   over-the-horizon
      across-the-beach capability and an amphibious
      evacuation capability.

LST   All three LSTs available had AAVs embarked.
      AAVs would provide a capability to move forces
      and   evacuees   across   a   beach   in   a   semi-
      permissive environment.

The orders stated that the Amphibious Forces should plan on the assumption that they would operate in a semi-permissive environment. In other words, there was the possibility of low-intensity opposition to their operations.

Vice Admiral Stanley Arthur tasked Rear Admiral John B. "Bat" LaPlante, commander of Amphibious Forces, with the planning of the operation and the proposing of a contingency task force to execute the mission. Rear Admiral LaPlante summoned PHIBRON 6 Commander Captain Alan B. Moser to a meeting on his flagship, the Amphibious Assault Ship USS Nassau (LHA 4). Having limited knowledge of conditions "on the ground" in Mogadishu, the two commanders envisioned a force capable of performing missions across the entire range of amphibious operations, including both surface and air actions. In addition to identifying the necessary amphibious ships and Marines for the mission, they proposed the assignment of two destroyers, which could provide fire support and electronic warfare capability should that become necessary. Despite the irregular nature of the fighting in Mogadishu, amphibious commanders were seriously concerned that sophisticated weapons systems might be present, particularly within the government faction. During much of the 1970s, Somalia had been a Cold War ally of the Soviet Union and had received both modern weapons and advisers. The relationship had soured and the Soviets had eventually withdrawn their support, but American commanders heeded to the possibility that Cold War weapons – especially surface-to-air missiles and electronic warfare equipment – remained in Somali's hands and could threaten their rescue mission. Rear Admiral LaPlante therefore recommended a seven-ship response force – four amphibious ships, two destroyer escorts, and one oiler – to conduct the operation, which was under Moser's command.

Vice Admiral Stanley Arthur recognized the importance of rescuing Americans in Somalia, but did not want to send seven ships to do the job. He viewed the action as strictly an extraction operation to get people out of and away from Mogadishu. There would be no ongoing operation ashore in Somalia or afloat in the Indian Ocean. At least Vice Admiral Arthur hoped to limit the mission to that role, because he needed all his ships for Desert Shield and Desert Storm – including the critical Sea Soldier IV workup. Commander, United States Navy, Central Command (Comusnavcent) knew that war with Iraq was inevitable absent a diplomatic solution. They did not want to divert more forces from the theater than was absolutely necessary. Vice Admiral Arthur feared that any forces sent to Somalia would be lost to him for an extended period of time. Once the ships were sent out of the operational area, Vice Admiral Arthur and his commanders knew getting them back could be a problem. For example, the evacuees coming out of Mogadishu would require transfer to a safe port. Could he bring them back to Oman, or would he have to send his ships to other locations – such as Mombasa, Kenya or the Island of Diego Garcia – even farther from the scene of action? Not wanting to degrade combat readiness in the Arabian Sea and Persian Gulf any more than absolutely necessary, Vice Admiral Arthur decided that a two-ship Amphibious Task Force with the right mix of helicopters and Marines could accomplish the mission in Mogadishu. Also involved in his consideration was the belief that additional forces could be sent later if necessary.

Two of the Amphibious ships at anchorage near Masirah, Oman – the USS Guam (LPH-9) and the USS Trenton (LPD 14) – not only had the necessary configuration but also were located nearest to the horn of Africa. Rear Admiral LaPlante assigned these two ships to conduct the rescue operation and sent PHIBRON 6 Commander Captain Al Moser – whom he held in high esteem and hated to lose – to act as commodore of the Amphibious Task Force. After meeting with Rear Admiral LaPlante aboard the USS Nassau (LHA-4) still in port at Dubai, Captain Al Moser took five members of his squadron staff and four officers from tactical air control squadron 12 and boarded a P-3 orion patrol aircraft for transport to an airport in Masirah, Oman that was the nearest to the USS Guam and USS Trenton. From there they would helicopter to the USS Guam. Concurrent with Rear Admiral LaPlante's planning, 4th Marine expeditionary Brigade Commander Marine Major General Harry Jenkins considered issues relating to the landing force that would conduct the rescue operation on the ground. He tasked Colonel James J. Doyle, Jr., the commander of brigade service support group 4, who was embarked on the USS Trenton, to serve as commander of the rescue mission to Mogadishu. Major General Jenkins instructed Colonel Doyle to create a special-purpose command element – designated 4th MEB, detachment 1 – aboard the amphibious assault ship and helicopter carrier USS Guam (LPH-9) to plan the operation and exercise command and control during its execution. The Rescue Force's departure was delayed by about eight to ten hours awaiting the augmentees from PHIBRON 6 and TACRON 22.

Colonel Doyle relocated from the USS Trenton to the USS Guam, bringing with him several key members of his brigade service support Group 4 staff, which he integrated with Marine officers from various headquarter elements to create an even more experienced, professional group. Equally important, the USS Guam's commanding officer Captain Charles R. Saffel, Jr. and the

Marine commander of troops aboard the Guam, Lieutenant Colonel Robert P. McAleer, along with their staffs, began planning for the operation even before the arrival of Colonel Doyle and Captain Moser. Once the two commander's helicopter aboard the USS Guam with their own skeleton staffs, they could take advantage of work already advanced. The officers, now assembled on board the USS Guam to plan and execute the rescue mission, had considerable experience in this type of operation. This was a collaborative effort among Navy and Marine officers who knew their jobs and knew their doctrine and procedures. When the USS Guam and USS Trenton received the warning and execution order to proceed to Mogadishu, the ships were positioned in the North Arabian Sea off the coast of Masirah, Oman approximately 1,500 miles from Mogadishu. On the bridge of the USS Guam, the Navy's navigation team had plotted the course and knew exactly how long it would take the ship to reach East Africa. You could feel the huge ship turning directions in the water. On the bridge of the Guam, commands were being barked out and repeated back to the bridge officer.

The USS Guam and USS Trenton proceeded south out of the North Arabian Sea at flank speed toward the Somalia capital of Mogadishu. The USS Guam vibrated as it plunged forward through the sea's water at flank speed. As the ships moved southward, Colonel Doyle and Captain Moser worked to organize their efforts. They quickly decided to create a combined command center in Guam's Supporting Arms Coordination Center (SACC). A contingency Marine air ground task force (MAGTF) was formed.

Table 6. Contingency MAGTF Organization Forces Available

CE   Command element (CE) comprised of 4TH MEB DET ONE staff, and detachments from: 2D SRIG, 8th Comm BN, 2D Intel CO, and 2D Recon CO. Commander was Col. J.J. Doyle (CO, BSSG-4).

GCE   Consisted of a HQS Company, a rifle company, and 81 mm mortar Platoon from BLT 1/2. Potential augmentation of seven to nine provisional rifle Platoons from the CE, CSSE, and ACE. Commander was Lieutenant Colonel R.P. McAleer (CO, BLT 1/2).

ACE   Consisted of HMM-263 (12 CH-46s), HMM-365 (12 CH-46s, MWSS-274, det. HMLA-269 (2 UH-1s armed with 2.75 in rocket pods) and det HMH-461 (2 CH-53Es).The commander was Lieutenant Colonel R.J. Wallace (CO, HMM-263).

CSSE   Consisted of a headquarters (HQ) detachment, MP Platoon, a landing support Det. and a medical/dental section that would be responsible for ECC. Commander was Maj. W.N. Saunders (XO, BSSG-4).

Immediately, Commander Amphibious Task Force (CATF), Commander Landing Force (CLF) and their staffs began to work out options. On the morning of 3 January

1991, the problems with the information about Mogadishu aboard the Guam became clear as the Phibron staff compared their Mogadishu map with the force's capabilities. They questioned why they had not been given an across-the-beach option and requested that an LST be added to the force. All three LSTs had amphibious assault vehicles (AAVs) embarked. They would provide the capability to move forces and evacuees across a beach in a semi-permissive environment. NAVCENT denied their request. Colonel Doyle brought with him from the USS Trenton a warrant officer who had served with the Marine security guard (MSG) detachment at Mogadishu in the mid-1980s. He proved his value when he looked at the map and material, and questioned its accuracy. He informed the planning staffs that he believed the US Embassy had been moved from the location shown because a new Compound had been planned and had been under construction several years earlier. That morning in discussions with CINCCENT, the Phibron Operations Officer (N3) confirmed this error and got the new Embassy Compound's grid coordinates. After confirming that the new Compound was far inland (not in Central Mogadishu), the planners felt their options were greatly reduced.

An over-the-beach evacuation was not sensible because the forces might have to fight their way across town. Thus, the only option was the use of helicopters; the question was whether to use CH-53Es or CH-46s. As the CH-46 has a very limited range and cannot be refueled in flight, the CH-53E would be the only option until the ships arrived off the coast of Mogadishu. Under the initial planning, the two ships wouldn't reach the CH-46 launch point until 062200 Zulu, or early in the morning on 7

January 1991 local time. There was initially, therefore, a four-day period in which the CH-53E option was the only means with which to conduct the rescue mission from the sea. Immediately upon notice, the Delta HMH-461 Detachment aboard the USS Trenton reported that they would be ready on three hours notice for insertion of the Rescue Force (as long as refueling could be coordinated). In the early morning hours on 3 January 1991, the crews of the two CH-53E Super Stallions from HMH-461 were briefed and began preparing for their mission into Mogadishu. On the afternoon of 3 January 1991, the two Super Stallion helicopters were fitted with refueling probes which had been removed due to shipboard space limitations, and two .50 caliber machine-guns were mounted. No one expected that US Navy ships would be sprinting down to the US Embassy in East Africa.

It had been over a year since the helicopter pilots practiced refueling, not having anticipated any such requirement during Operation Desert Shield and Desert Storm. The CH-53E's Super Stallions helicopters are designed to conduct in-flight refueling; they have a long-range insertion capability and remain the only US heavy-lift helicopter that can fly into an uncertain environment at long distances. Available for Operation Eastern Exit were three crews for the aircraft. As the planners began working on preparing a Rescue Force to insert into the US Embassy Compound, the uppermost question was the threat they might face. The intelligence was unclear concerning both the threat and the situation in Mogadishu. The US Embassy and all foreign embassies were on 100% alert and had also been in constant communication with their senior officials located in their countries.

In the evening on 3 January 1991, US Embassy buildings were hit by 10-15 rounds of machine-gun fire. In the city of Mogadishu, artillery fire was thundering, plumes of smoke marked impacts to the southeast, small arms fire was everywhere, and looting was becoming more widespread. Ambassador James K. Bishop received messages from several diplomatic colleagues asking for rescue and/or refuge. The response to each was that he and his staff were welcome, but the US Embassy could not mount any rescue operations. After contacting their senior officials in their respective countries, each foreign Embassy were ordered to pack what they could, destroy all confidential and classified documents, evacuate the Compound, and make their way to the US Embassy the best way they could. All foreign embassies in Mogadishu were now in what would become known as their most desperate hours. At each foreign Embassy, the ambassadors with their staffs, personnel and their families (including little children) frantically packed what they could carry, as well as shredded and burned all confidential and classified documents. There was a lot of fear as each foreign Embassy prepared to evacuate their Compound. They could hear the crackling of machine-gun fire mingled with the dull thuds of rocket-propelled grenade rounds as they impacted on buildings somewhere in the near distance. Many of the children were frightened and were asking their parents if they were going to be safe. One little girl said to her mother, *"Mommy I'm scared; nothing bad is going to happen to us, is it?"* The mother comforted her little daughter and told her they were going to be okay; they just had to leave the country. No one wanted to fall into the hands of corrupt government soldiers, African Rebel Forces or armed looters. The foreign embassies with their personnel would take advantage of lulls in firing using the most safe, strategic route to make their way to the US Compound in their commercial vehicles.

Late on 3 January 1991, the Rescue Force began direct contact with the US Embassy, sending an Element of Essential Information (EEI) list of questions. Contacts with the US Embassy were limited by several problems. First, the Embassy reportedly had few uplinks working and was required to maintain voice contact with the State Department in Washington D.C. until the morning of 4 January 1991. Second, there was no common crypto material for the Embassy and the ships so that when direct voice communication became possible, it was in the clear. The fact that all voice communications were transmitted in the clear greatly limited the amount and type of information that could be passed over the radio between the US Embassy and the forces aboard the USS Guam; secure communication occurred via state department cable and Navy message traffic. Some means were used to get around this restriction when possible. For example, the US Embassy requested that the top ten questions be listed from the 42-item EEI list so that they could be answered immediately. The numbers were provided over the radio, and these questions were answered by message traffic almost within the hour. By late afternoon on 4 January 1991, the full set of questions had been answered.

After receiving authority to exceed the CH-53 peacetime passenger restriction of 18, an 80-man Rescue Force was outlined to be inserted into the US Embassy (40 on each CH-53E). The basic requirements for the Rescue Force calls for three different organizations on the ground: 1) the forward command element (FCE) which will include the ground commander who will liaison with the US ambassador and a communications team; 2) a ground combat element (GCE), which is to provide security during the evacuation; and 3) an evacuation control center (ECC), which is responsible for processing evacuees. The 80-man Rescue Force included both Marines and Navy Seals. Since this was a mixed force, it was one of the few areas of disagreement between Commander Amphibious Task Force (CATF) and Commander Landing Force (CLF). We agreed to disagree. CLF questioned the requirement for including the Seal Team, because the Marines and Navy Seals that would make up the Rescue Force had not worked together before and did not know each other. CATF felt that the close quarter warfare (CQW) training of the Navy Seals would be useful on the ground in Mogadishu, and that the two groups (Seals and Marines) would thus compliment each other's capabilities. As CATF commands in an amphibious operation, both Seals and Marines were included in the Rescue Force. CG Fourth MEB then required the force to be reduced to no more than 30 men on each helicopter. Reductions included a ten-man cut in the GCE, removing two of three members of the ECC, and eliminating the two-member combat camera team from the operation. The reduction in the size of the GCE was made reluctantly because there was a feeling that the Rescue Force was at a minimum size to execute the mission.

By late afternoon on 4 January 1991, the long range CH-53E insertion of the Rescue Force was a definite GO! Coordinating the in-flight refueling for the CH-53E was now a priority. Vice Admiral Stanley Arthur had earlier contacted US Air Force representatives at Central Command and learned that they could not provide tanker support due to other commitments. He then contacted

Major General Royal N. Moore, commanding general of the 3rd Marine Aircraft Wing, and arranged for Marine Corps KC-130 tankers to refuel the CH-53E Super Stallions. One of the more difficult problems faced was coordinating flight times between the USMC KC-130s and the CH-53Es that they would refuel in-flight on the way to Mogadishu.

Three KC-130s from VMGR-252 and VMGR-352 departed Bahrain shortly before 1300z for an airfield closer to Mogadishu (with an ETA of 1430z), where they would assume a two-hour alert posture. On board the USS Guam was only one Marine Rifle Company, Charlie Company 1st Battalion 2nd Marines. None of the non-commissioned officers from Charlie Company, who were chosen for the rescue mission, had been notified yet.

On the afternoon of 4 January, the majority of the Marines from Charlie Company were in the Company sleeping quarters after eating lunch waiting for our 1300 formation. Many of us were watching television while other Marines were writing letters and reading books. Earlier, we had felt the ship changing directions in the sea and plunging through the waters at flank speed. But everyone assumed it was just maneuvers. On 4 January 1991 early in the evening, I was on the lower level of the Guam doing laundry when my Platoon Sergeant, Staff Sergeant J. Cox, walked in and said *"Corporal LaLand, I need you upstairs right now; we have an emergency meeting with the Platoon commander. There is a critical crisis at the US Embassy in East Africa"*. I'm thinking what does Africa have to do with us? We were preparing for the Gulf War and the coming assault on Kuwait to physically remove and destroy the Iraqi Army in that city. When I arrived upstairs in our sleeping quarters, the rest of my Platoon was there. Two minutes later, our Platoon commander, 2nd Lieutenant H.R. VanOpdorp walked in and began to brief us. *"The USS Guam and USS Trenton have been ordered to leave the Kuwait Theater of Operations and proceed 1500 miles south to the capitol of Somalia Africa, Mogadishu to rescue the besieged US Embassy and foreign nationals who are trapped in that city by the violent Civil War. Two reinforced squads from our Platoon (2nd and 3rd squads) and two reinforced squads from 3rd Platoon along with the Platoon commanders, Platoon sergeants, company commander, 1 Navy Corpsman and our Battalion commander as well as a nine-man Navy Seal Team, will be the rescue team. The Rescue Force will also include a two-man sniper team in which Sergeant Jennings from our Platoon will be detached out as a sniper and spotter for the mission, and there will be one Forward Air Control (FAC) Officer who will call in an airstrike from an AC-130 specter gunship providing fire support if needed. Corporal LaLand, you will be the radio man for the FAC officer in which you will be carrying the PRC 113 Radio. Our mission is to rescue and secure the US Embassy and evacuate American and foreign nationals from the Compound once the USS Guam and USS Trenton arrive off the coast of Mogadishu.*

We will fly ahead of the ships, over water at night by two CH-53E Super Stallion helicopters in which the choppers will be refueled in air by Marine KC-130 tankers staged in Nairobi, Kenya in order to have enough fuel to reach the Embassy. At this point, we are not exactly sure when the Rescue Force will launch for Mogadishu. But we are looking at a 4-6 hour flight with at least 2-4 in-flight refueling all over water and during the night. The nine-man Navy Seal Team will be on our chopper. We will draw our ammunition on the hangar bay and receive further briefing by the company commander there. Any questions....if not, everybody cowboy up and meet me on the hangar bay in five minutes." I had on my PT shorts and running shoes. So I had to quickly change into my desert-camouflaged fatigues and put my boots on. At the present time, no one was talking. Our call to spring into action came. We knew what we had to do, and we were serious.

Everyone "Cowboyed" up grabbing rifles, bayonets, H-harness, helmets, packs, and their night vision gear (NVGs). After every Marine had all their gear on, we began walking up the ladderwell (stairwell) coming from our sleeping quarters and headed towards the hangar bay. When the four reinforced squads from Charlie Company had assembled in the hangar bay, our company commander Captain Dysart further briefed us. *"Men, we are responding to a critical situation that is deteriorating fast which you have been briefed on by your Platoon commander. Lives are at stake and the call for help has come to us, and we are going to answer the call, in force. The tensions in the civil war-torn East African nation of Somalia have turned into a blood bath resulting in the destruction of several foreign embassies, and the American Embassy is in great danger of following suit. Ambassadors and their personnel from many foreign countries have sought refuge and rescue at the US Embassy Compound while other foreign Embassy's are still trapped at their Compounds in the city. The initial plans called for the evacuation of the endangered Americans through Mogadishu's international airport, utilizing air force aircraft staged in Kenya. But the situation in Mogadishu has rapidly deteriorated. And aircraft, even those of the US Air Force, cannot land safely at the airport.*

Everyone sheltered at the Embassy would not be able to travel safely through the embattled city to the airport. And on top of all that all telephone lines are down in the city, and there is absolutely no communication with Mogadishu's airport personnel. There has been a lot of emergency planning and briefings in such a short period of time because of the urgency of the crisis. Colonel James J. Doyle BSSG-4 is the commander of landing forces that has been formed from the 4th Marine Expeditionary Brigade. The two, CH-53E Super Stallions will carry a 60-man Rescue Force consisting of forty-seven Marines from Charlie Company commanded by our battalion commander Lieutenant Colonel McAleer, four Marines from Colonel Doyle's brigade service support group 4 headquarters element, and nine Navy Seals under Commander Stephen R. Louma USN. Lieutenant Colonel Willard Oats will be the overall commander of the forward element. He will be the senior officer on the ground in Mogadishu, working primarily with the American ambassador after arriving at the US Embassy.

Major William N. Saunders will serve as the logistician for the mission, specifically supervising the Evaluation Control Center (ECC) which will process evacuees and prepare them for departure. Once the choppers touch-down in the Compound, the Navy Seal Team will run straight for the Chancery Building to concentrate on protecting the American ambassador and augmenting the five Marine security guards (MSG) who are stationed there. Charlie Company will secure the Compound set in a defensive perimeter to defend the Compound. The two-man sniper team will set up a position on the water tower. The American ambassador has recently stated that all hope is fading fast; Men, their only hope of rescue lays with us. We are Marines, and we are not going to fail them. If there are no questions, we will start drawing ammunition in five minutes and then wait for word to move up to the flight deck."

Our ammunition began arriving on the elevator from the belly of the ship by way of Navy personnel with forklifts. We cracked open the crates of ammo and started passing it out. I had four fragmentation hand grenades, 500 5.56 rounds for my M16 A2 rifle, 24 rounds for my M203 grenade launcher, which included 40mm high explosives (HE), smoke illumination rounds, and CS gas, one light anti-tank weapon (LAW) and the PRC 113 radio. Due to the uncertain threat, we were going in heavily armed and loaded with everything we could carry, with almost every man carrying some form of automatic weapon and anti-tank weapon (which included dragons, light anti-armor weapons (LAAWs), and AT-4s). With all the weapons, ammunition and equipment each Marine was carrying, our combat load was well over 125 pounds. Everything we carried was heavy, but we were trained and physically fit to carry these heavy combat loads. We were prepared to battle and even had our bayonets attached to our cartridge belts just in case we were to engage in hand-to-hand combat. Both senior officers Lieutenant Colonel Oats and Lieutenant Colonel McAleer who would normally just carry a 9mm pistol were both carrying M16 A2 rifles in addition to their 9mm pistols. CLF and CAF included a large contingent of officers in the Rescue Force because they wanted senior officers on the ground in Mogadishu.

Colonel Doyle stated that sending two lieutenant colonels, one Navy commander, and a major in addition to the normal complement of officers and non-commissioned officers seemed excessively top heavy, but Colonel Doyle considered this "an unconventional operation with potentially extraordinary consequences" and wanted a "few guys with gray hair" in the landing zone. Loss of American life in the US Embassy at Mogadishu would distract the nation as it approached the critical point of war in the Persian Gulf. Additionally, Colonel Doyle clearly remembered the Iranian hostage crisis, when on 4 November 1979; Iranian militants stormed the US Embassy in Tehran, taking American personnel and US Marine security guards hostage for the next 444 days. The American hostages faced many hardships and suffered at the hands of their captors.

Either scenario could unhinge Desert Shield and Desert Storm planning, resulting in unthinkable consequences. Colonel Doyle organized the Rescue Force in a Marine air-ground task force structure. In Colonel Doyle's organizational plan, Lieutenant Colonel Oats would function as the senior officer on the ground in Mogadishu, although McAleer held the same rank and would command most of the Marines. Fortunately, command issues would not be a problem despite the large number of high-ranking officers that made up part of the 60-man Rescue Force, because Lieutenant Colonel Oats and Lieutenant Colonel McAleer tended to be of one mind throughout the mission.

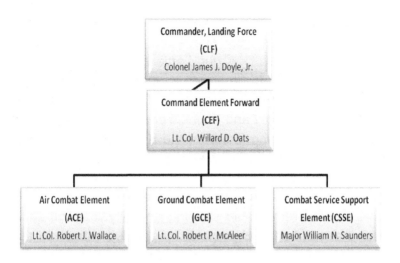

On the ground in Mogadishu, 4 January 1991 was by far the worst day. A Soviet aircraft attempted to fly into Mogadishu airport from Aden, Yemen to evacuate their people from war-torn Somalia, but was unable to land as well as Italian military aircraft from the 46th Air Brigade, that attempted to fly into the airport from Nairobi, Kenya but their attempt failed also. Early on 4 January 1991, the US Embassy learned that looters armed with AK-47 assault rifles had breached the 160-acre US Compound. Half of the US Embassy's 160-acre Compound was a primitive 80-acre golf course. The internal wall separating the recreation area from the Chancery, Marine House Residence, and JAO Complex was perforated like the wall on Afgoy Road, every 20 yards by 2-foot gaps blocked by thin bars. Normally the US Embassy would not have to worry about anything more lethal than wild dogs coming through the gaps. The armed looters who breached the US Embassy Compound were trashing the golf course and terrifying the FSN families safe-havened there. US Embassy guards were dispatched to the golf course to deal with the intruders. When they arrived at the golf course, they fired warning shots over the heads of the armed looters when more subtle means of chasing them off were unsuccessful. A gun battle erupted between US Embassy guards and the armed looters. In the exchange of fire, several armed looters were killed. Both sides then withdrew. Bob Noble and Elaine York were two of the US Embassy guards who fought in the brief gun battle. Bob Noble was a former special air services trooper who was always at the point of maximum danger. Elaine York was on her first tour abroad as a security officer. She demonstrated remarkable stamina and physical courage. After the gun battle, Bob Noble negotiated with a militia commander whom he had befriended for armed help in fighting off any other golf course looters, and protecting the FSN families who were safe-havened there. While Bob was talking to the militia commander, Somali government soldiers broke into the K-7 Compound and seized US Embassy personnel Bill Mueller and Chris Swenson. They released Bill and Chris when they gave them the keys to one of the vehicles in the courtyard. Bill and Chris Swenson then retreated to a safe haven, while the Somali soldiers helped themselves to the US Embassy vehicles at the K-7 Compound. Back at the Chancery Compound, commercial officer Mike Shanklin, a retired Marine officer, armed him self and took an armored van to evacuate everyone to the Chancery from the glass-walled residence now in the line of fire of any looters on the golf course. The US Embassy guards and staff then buttoned up the Chancery and the JAO headquarters which were the main safe-haven buildings. The US Embassy sent a series of flash messages to Washington D.C. alerting them of their situation.

On board the USS Guam and USS Trenton, it had become essential that the ships close the distance to Mogadishu as fast as possible. The Guam had a top speed of twenty-four knots, whereas the Trenton could make about eighteen knots maximum. There was no requirement to keep the ships together, and initially the USS Guam steamed at near maximum speed, outpacing the USS Trenton by four nautical miles an hour. The question of when to launch the Rescue Force remained under discussion, but Ambassador Bishop's urgent messages forced the issue into the forefront. The potential launch point had varied as the ships steamed south. Colonel Doyle and Captain Moser had considered launching the helicopters directly from their initial positions in the Northern Arabian Sea, some 1500 miles from the target area. They again considered it when the ships reached a point 890 miles away, but ultimately the decision was made to launch the helicopters once the USS Guam reached a distance of 466 nautical miles from Mogadishu.

In addition to Ambassador Bishop's distressed calls for help, a number of issues contributed to the decision to launch the helicopters at this juncture, including in-flight refueling requirements, the availability of tanker support, the arrival time over Mogadishu, and the availability of AC-130 gunships to provide cover. The Marine CH-53E pilots who would fly the mission felt that in order to improve the chance of mission success, a mission less than 500 nautical miles was preferable due to lowered in-flight refueling requirements, and a dawn/daylight arrival in Mogadishu would facilitate insertion of the Rescue Force.

Launching beyond 466 miles could multiply problems that the pilots might face in conducting a long-range insertion due to the additional refueling requirements. Conversely, waiting for a closer launch point would very likely prove disastrous for the Embassy personnel, as local conditions continued to worsen. The two CH-53E Super Stallion helicopters flying the mission were assigned to the USS Trenton. On 4 January 1991 at 1815 hrs, they departed Trenton and flew ahead to cross-deck on the USS Guam, carrying with them the nine Navy Seals and Major Saunders, the ECC officer who was also assigned to the Trenton. They would join the rest of the Rescue Force and await the order to launch for Mogadishu. Once on board Guam, the CH-53E crews conducted final flight planning and received intelligence briefings. Threats to the aircraft included SA-2 and SA-3 missiles, both high-altitude surface-to-air missiles (SAMS), and many anti-aircraft artillery (AAA) guns throughout the city. The SAM threat led to a decision to make a low altitude ingress to the US Embassy Compound on arrival in Mogadishu. The flight crews who had been awake since 0500 hrs would retire at 2000 hrs for crew rest, the TACRON personnel would schedule the aerial refueling control points (ARCP), and coordinate the KC-130 Marine tankers.

At the US Embassy, the armed looters returned back to the golf course. Bob Noble's militiamen came to the rescue, chasing the looters off the golf course in a brisk exchange of fire. Bill Mueller and Chris Swenson, who were released by Somalia government soldiers, made it back to the Embassy Compound once the soldiers departed the K-7 area. Bill and Chris were replaced later as lookouts by Matt Kula, who kept watch from a trap door on top of the water tower until it came under fire later, on 4 January 1991. In addition to small-arms impacts inside the

US Embassy Compound, a rocket-propelled grenade, probably aimed at the water tower, struck a warehouse near the JAO safe haven, terrifying the Americans and foreign nationals inside. At the US Embassy Gate 1 Combat Consuls, Brian Phipps, Mark Manning, and John Fox dressed in flack-jackets, ducked bullets as they decided who to admit into the Compound for evacuation. These were painful decisions made in a tense and emotional environment, but all three performed superbly.

An American woman who was a private citizen showed up at the US Embassy Gate 1. She had been shot in the abdomen. It was unclear to the US Embassy staff how she became wounded. But they all assumed she had been the victim of a robbery, because many people were getting shot and killed by armed looters in the city of Mogadishu. Also along with this American woman, the Sudanese Ambassador's wife who was nine months pregnant miraculously showed up at the US Embassy Gate 1. They were both crying and very emotional. They were treated by Karen McGuire Rugh and the US Embassy contract physician. The American woman was in stable condition but would need surgery immediately to remove the bullet lodged in her abdomen. By now, the heads of 10 foreign diplomatic missions with their staff and families had made it to the US Embassy for shelter and rescue. Several chiefs of mission had been beaten and robbed by uniformed looters. US Ambassador James K. Bishop spoke with his staff and Embassy guards privately, telling them, *"We cannot predict how much longer Bob's militiamen will stand guard at the golf course, and Somalia government soldiers' violation of the K-7 Compound has clearly put us in greater jeopardy. We certainly cannot count on remaining unmolested until the scheduled arrival of the Marines in two days. With that said I'm going to contact Washington D.C. informing them that the situation is very critical and fragile, and that we need immediate help."*

Ambassador Bishop then makes another distress call to Washington as his staff looks on, communicating a rather desperate requirement for immediate assistance. He stated that the US Embassy was falling behind the curve in their ability to protect themselves from the lawlessness which now prevails in Mogadishu – recommend immediate airlift from Saudi Arabia of a US parachute force sufficient to provide augmented security to the Chancery and JAO Building where everyone currently is safe-havened. He felt that two Platoons would be sufficient, but Washington denied the request. This was not the answer Ambassador Bishop was looking for, with so many lives under his watch. He felt that surely among 240,000 American troops deployed to the Gulf, there was two Platoons who could be put in position to provide assistance before the task force arrived in timeframe shorter than 27 hours. Clearly, the Ambassador felt the situation on the ground in Mogadishu was getting desperate for the Americans and foreign nationals sheltered in the US Embassy Compound. No American ambassador wants to be put in a predicament where he has to make a decision to surrender his Embassy staff and personnel to violent militants or rebel forces, because he does not know what his fate or the fate of his staff and personnel will be. No doubt this weighed heavily on Ambassador Bishop's mind, for he knew that African rebels and militants were brutal. They are known to cut off limbs, cut off women's breasts, cut out the babies of pregnant women, and mutilate people in other ways. Just the thought of this brings a cold chill down your spine.

When the task force on board the USS Guam received the message that Ambassador Bishop requested that two Platoons of US paratroopers be dropped to protect Americans until the Amphibious Task Force could arrive, Colonel Doyle and other commanders considered it a bad idea because the space available for a drop zone was so small that paratroopers might be scattered outside the Embassy Compound, as well as possibly be shot as they came down. Such an operation also increased the number of people requiring evacuation. More important, by the time Ambassador Bishop made his request, events had out-paced its rationale; the task force was nearing the position to launch its helicopters with the 60-man Rescue Force sooner than Ambassador Bishop had expected. And the Rescue Force would likely arrive before paratroops could be delivered.

After high level meetings in Washington DC, Ambassador Bishop was informed that advance elements of Marines and Navy Seals would reach the US Embassy at dawn the following day, 5 January 1991. Ambassador Bishop talked with his staff and Embassy guards telling them that, *"We must hold the Compound until the Rescue Force arrives at dawn tomorrow. All Embassy guards will be on 100% alert all night guarding the perimeter and keeping a high visibility. The communication staff will man the phone lines through the night."*

As the sun began to set and darkness drew near, no other foreign nationals had arrived at the American Compound. Ambassador Bishop instructed his communication staff to make contact with foreign diplomats still trapped in the city at their Compounds, to advise them not to make an attempt to travel to the US Embassy because darkness will soon cover the city. But they should wait until tomorrow when the US Rescue Force arrives. Ambassador Bishop walked over to the Chancery and the JAO Building to talk with everyone sheltered inside which now exceeded 500. Upon arriving, he asked could he have everyone's attention. He encouraged them to stay hopeful and informed them that advance elements of the Rescue Force will be arriving earlier than expected. At dawn tomorrow, a combined 60-man Rescue Force of US Marines and Navy Seals will arrive in the Compound by ship-based helicopters from the Amphibious Task Force. They will help us defend the Compound until the task force ships arrive off the coast to evacuate us which will be sometime after midnight on 6 January. Ambassador Bishop's words brought cheers and smiles to many faces, but not to everyone. Somali foreign service nationals (FSNs) and Somali hired guards knew that they would not be evacuated with everyone else, and began asking Ambassador Bishop nervous questions about their safety and future. Ambassador Bishop answered their questions to the best of his ability, knowing their future was uncertain.

On board the USS Guam, CINCCENT issued the final execute order late in the evening, 4 January 1991, with a launch time of 0247 hrs on 5 January. With this launch time, the Rescue Force would arrive at 0720 hrs shortly after dawn in Mogadishu. On the hangar bay of the Guam, the Rescue Force had been waiting for several hours for the green light to go. It had been a long wait. We were all gathered in a tight group in a small section of the hangar bay leaning back on our packs. In our eyes, we had the look of confidence and there was no fear. We knew we had each other's backs. The nine-man Navy Seal Team was located in a secluded area of the ship. By now, our mood was laid back and relaxed waiting for the word to go. There was some small chatter among us. Some Marines talked about their girlfriends and wives and what it will be like to see them again. Other Marines talked about the mission anticipating what we might expect when we reached the US Embassy, while other Marines were in their own world thinking to themselves. I personally was thinking about my family and my girlfriend Janice, and the last two days of quiet time she and I shared together before I was deployed for the war. At 0145 hrs, the CH-53E crews awoke for weather, intelligence, the latest navigational information, and mission briefings. At 0200 hrs from the bridge of the Guam, the Rescue Force received the green light to move up to the flight deck to board the choppers. We began to make our way up the stairwell leading to the flight deck.

Over the ship's radio, you hear the command *"flight quarters, flight quarters, all hands man your flight quarter stations."* When we arrived on the flight deck, the nine Navy Seals were already there and the helicopters were still shut down and had not turned their power on yet, but the pilots were already inside. We received a short briefing from the senior crew chief before loading. As I stood there, I looked at the full bright moon reflecting off the night ocean, and I recalled all the times I would come on the flight deck at night with fellow Marines from my Platoon, where we would just sit down, talk, and enjoy the beautiful view. But now I'm on the flight deck at night preparing to go on a drastic rescue mission into hostile territory. After the briefing, we loaded onto the helicopters. The Seal Team was on the same helicopter my Platoon was on.

They loaded first and positioned themselves at the rear of the chopper placing their weapons and packs in the middle of the floor. With our heavy load, this caused us to climb over their gear to reach the seats to the front. The Seals should have loaded last and allowed the Marines to load first. As me and Corporal Jenkins were getting on the helicopter, one of the Navy Seals had his boots completely in our way. We both stopped and looked at the Seal without saying anything, but the expressions on our faces was saying, *"Man move your boot!"* He knew why we stopped and was looking at him, and he did move his boots out of the way. The last thing we needed was friction between the Navy Seals and the Marines. We were going in as a US military force on the same team, just different branches of service. If we got into a "firefight" in Africa, we were going to fight side by side. But regardless of the loading sequence, we were all spread-load on the CH-53E Super Stallions with every seat filled and all our packs with anti-tank weapons in the middle of the floor. Each helicopter carried one Marine Platoon, the Seal Team, and at least one of the senior officers. If either helicopter crashed or otherwise couldn't reach Mogadishu, which was viewed as a very real possibility, the mission could still go ahead. In this event, the decision to go ahead would rest with Major Dan Schultz, the senior officer flying the mission (who was the officer in charge of the HMH-461 detachment), as well as Lieutenant Colonel W.D. Oats, the FCE commander.

Colonel Doyle and Captain Moser specifically avoided trying to create specific "no-go" criteria and instead left such a decision with the on-scene commanders. My Platoon was on the lead helicopter that would be flown by Major Dan Schultz and his co-pilot. I looked to the front where the pilots were sitting and you could see them flipping the illuminated panels' switches and turning the engines power on. The illuminated panel lights glared on the pilots' green flight suits and gloves like chem-lights glowing in the dark.

You could hear and feel the thrush of power from the CH-53E engine. We began to rock back and forth in our seats from the power of those enormous rotor blades whipping up.

We were now just waiting for the green light from the Guam's command center to launch. The Guam's commanding officer, Captain Saffell was also an aviator. He was acutely attuned to the problems and risks of night-time refueling over an open ocean. He delayed the helicopter launch until he had a visual of the KC-130s on radar. Once there was a visual of the KC-130s, he would track both groups to ensure a rendezvous was successful. At 0245 hrs, Captain Saffell stated, *"I have a visual of KC-130 tankers on radar."* Captain Al Moser then spoke the command "Execute Operation Eastern Exit". Colonel Doyle repeated the command in his headset which was relayed to the pilots. The command "Execute Operation Eastern Exit" echoed in the headsets of the pilots. They responded saying Roger "Execute Operation Eastern Exit". The lights on the flight deck of the Guam went from red to yellow to green. One Navy flight deck crewman standing in front of each CH-53E Super Stallion helicopter gave the hand and arm signal to launch.

At 0247 hrs on 5 January 1991 at a distance of 466 nautical miles from Mogadishu, the USS Guam launched the two CH-53E Super Stallion helicopters with the Rescue Force. Almost immediately, the Omega Navigation Systems on both helicopters stopped providing navigation information, and neither aircraft was able to get more than two fixes. With some guidance from the Guam, the two CH-53Es headed south to the first aerial refueling control point (ARCP) using dead-reckoning for navigation. Meanwhile back at the US Embassy in Mogadishu, everyone was crowded into the Chancery and JAO Building. The Embassy staff talked through the night with the US Task Force approaching them, keeping them updated on the conditions on the ground in Mogadishu. Some of the many people sheltered in the US Compound were able to catch some sleep. But for others, it would be a restless night, not knowing if they would wake up to explosions and machine-gun fire in the Compound.

The Sudanese Ambassador embraced and comforted his wife who was pregnant and due any day. He kissed her on the forehead and said, *"Don't worry, everything will be alright. The U.S Marines and Navy Seals will be here soon.*

The two CH-53E helicopters were now close to the first aerial refueling control-point. The helicopters were flying at 6,000 feet, which is the altitude used for in-flight refueling. With machine-guns mounted on the doors, the cabin was exposed to the air at this altitude, and despite being near the Equator, the helicopters were quite cold. We were now at a distance of 185 nautical miles from the USS Guam, preparing to rendezvous with the KC-130 tanker planes. The crews of the KC-130s, which are not night vision goggle-capable (NVGs), were unable to see the CH-53Es as they approached, because the helicopters' formation lights were not visible from more than a mile away. The helicopter pilots and KC-130 pilots made radio contact with each other. As the pilots talked, the CH-53Es briefly turned on their spotlights so that the KC-130 tanker planes could see the helicopters. At this point, one of the Omega navigation aids became operational, and its accuracy was verified with one of the KC-130 navigators. The helicopter pilots would only use the Omega Navigation System as a backup for the mission.

To the west of the helicopters, you could see two KC-130 tanker planes slowly descend upon the two CH-53E Super Stallion helicopters like a dove. I was thinking to myself if anything went seriously wrong during the refueling and a helicopter crashed in the dark ocean at night, the chances of surviving the impact and crash would not be good. I began to pray to God that the refueling would be successful, and that the overall mission would be a success. The KC-130 pilots positioned their planes to the right of the helicopters just above the rotor blades. I observed the long hose mechanically released from the KC-130 tanker plane, which was guided around and expertly connected into the CH-53E helicopters. Both helicopters plugged successfully and began receiving fuel. This in-flight refueling was vital to the mission, for if it failed, the helicopters would be forced to return to the ships. The helicopters and the KC-130s maintain the same speed. We had been in the process of refueling for several minutes when all of a sudden, the fuel line in the helicopter I was riding developed a fuel leak. The JP-5 fuel began to pour in the troop compartment. The odor was very strong but not overwhelming. The fuel came into the troop compartment so fast that many of us did not have time to react. On top of that, we were still strapped into our seatbelts and there was hardly any room to move. I was able to move to my left just enough to avoid a heavy dousing of the fuel, but my team member Lance Corporal T.A. Dennis, who was sitting next to me, got doused pretty good. I could tell by the way he was grunting and by the look on his face that he was in some pain. The JP-5 fuel had gone down into the crouch of his pants, and it was burning him. He used a cloth with water from his canteen to wash the fuel off, but that wasn't good enough. He and the other Marines that had received a large dousing of fuel would need a shower. The Navy Seal Team at the rear of the helicopter did not receive a large dousing of the fuel. The crew chief worked frantically to repair the fuel line as Major Dan Schultz initiated an emergency break-away. The JP-5 fumes filled the compartment. After the crew chief successfully repaired the fuel line by using a large wrench to tighten the pipelines where the fuel was profusely leaking from, the aircraft re-plugged without further incident. The two CH-53E Super Stallion helicopters now had enough fuel to reach Mogadishu and the operation was a "Go".

Major Dan Shultz sent a message to the command center on the USS Guam, *"Command Center, this is Oscar 4 Sierra, first refueling successful, continuing on course to Mogadishu"*. The planners on board the USS Guam had been up many hours without sleep. They were going to stay awake to ensure the mission was a success. They had plenty of coffee in the command center. The leg to the second ARCP was 225 nautical miles. If this refueling failed, the two CH-53Es Super Stallion helicopters would fly to the US Embassy, insert the Rescue Force, and then fly into the desert where they would then wait for the USS Guam and USS Trenton to steam within range. We had now been in the air over three hours. The crack of dawn was beginning to break through the sky. We reached our second aerial refueling control point. Once again the two KC-130 tanker planes were to the west of us, and began to slowly descend upon the two helicopters like doves. This was a long flight for all of us.

The second refueling was completed on schedule and without any incidents. Both helicopters had taken on a total of 24,000 pounds of fuel in the two refueling. The second refueling ended with the helicopters just 53 nautical miles from the US Embassy. At this time, the KC-130s gave a last navigational fix to the helicopters, which then began a descent from 6,000 ft in preparation for a low-level insertion profile. The KC-130 tanker planes began a high-level orbit and established communications with the USS Guam. At 0630 hrs on the ground at the US Embassy, Marine security guards reported to US Ambassador James K. Bishop that about 250 armed African rebel soldiers had begun placing ladders on the Compound walls preparing for an assault. The American ambassador knew that the Embassy was in trouble, but he ordered the Embassy Marines and security personnel to hold their fire, and retreat back to the Chancery and JAO buildings, telling them the Rescue Force should be here shortly.

The two helicopters were just minutes away. At 0650 hrs, the crew chief on each helicopter test-fired the .50 caliber machine guns, firing the rounds into the ocean warning the Rescue Force to prepare for insertion. My Platoon commander, 2nd Lieutenant H.R. VanOpdorp yelled out, *"Lock and load your weapons"*. The Navy Seal Team adjusted their gear, prepped their weapons and stood up, getting into some type of comradeship formation with their left hand on each other's shoulders and holding their weapons in their right hand. As the pilots began their approach into Mogadishu, they picked up speed to avoid possible rocket-propelled grenades (RPG) and surfaced to air missiles that they were briefed on. Right at dawn, the two CH-53E Super Stallion helicopters crossed the coast at approximately 25 to 50 feet altitude, screaming in at 150 knots (175 mph) over the city of Mogadishu. The Super Stallion helicopters crossed the beach south of the harbor with the sun at their backs.

Marine Major Dan Schultz, flying the helicopter my Platoon was on, banked his Super Stallion helicopter hard left, and the rear helicopter carrying 3rd Platoon did the same. The pilots expertly flew their helicopters low over the city of Mogadishu. Major Schultz planned the ingress route around avoiding the major fighting, which was reported to be in the northern sections of the city and around the presidential palace near the harbor area. Based on the map on hand, the US Embassy Compound was clearly in an isolated area, and the pilots had been told it was distinguishable by its golf course and large white stucco Compound wall. In addition, there was to be a man waving a white flag marking the helicopter landing zone (HLZ). If navigating across part of the Indian Ocean had been difficult, locating the US Embassy proved equally vexing. The US Embassy Compound proved difficult to identify from the air, particularly at low altitude in the early morning light. As the pilots looked for the US Embassy, virtually every building seemed to have "a large white stucco fence" around it, and the pilots were unable to identify a golf course. This greatly increased the risk to the two helicopters because active combat was ongoing in the city. Even though the helicopters were flying very fast, the Rescue Force was still able to get a glimpse of the city through the small windows in the troop compartment. Off in the distance, we could see pillars of black smoke rising from the city. People were running around in disarray, and many of them were armed with weapons. I didn't see any animals or children, but Mogadishu definitely looked like a war-torn city.

After flying around the city for 10 to 15 minutes, Major Schultz pulled the Super Stallion helicopters back over the water to try his backup approach, which involved flying over the airport and then a one-minute and ten-second leg to the US Embassy Compound. On the way in the second time, the Super Stallion helicopters flew over a column of trucks including several mounting 12.7-mm AA guns. The Somalis jumped off their trucks and ran for cover as the helicopters approached. The helicopters established radio contact with the US Embassy in an attempt to get guidance to the Compound, but the radio operator was unable to provide assistance because he was in a windowless room. This was the first communication the US Embassy received from the helicopters indicating that they were actually inbound and at what time they would be arriving. Earlier contact had been avoided because it would have been in the clear and the risk of a security breach precluded such contact.

Within minutes, Major Dan Schultz and his co-pilot saw what they thought might be the US Embassy. They observed a large number of armed African Rebel Forces gathered with ladders by one wall and, reportedly, a large volume of gunfire was being directed into the Compound. As the two CH-53Es Super Stallion helicopters flew into the US Compound, they flew low over this gathering. The African Rebel Forces scattered like flies as they looked up in amazement and saw these two enormous helicopters swooping in low over them. As the Super Stallion helicopters crossed the Compound wall, a man came running out waving a white sheet to mark the helicopter landing zone. The helicopters simultaneously began to descend to the ground of the US Compound.

The wind from the helicopters' massive rotor blades was kicking up dirt, rocks and even blew down some of the ladders that the African Rebel Forces had placed on the US Embassy walls. Everyone safe-havened inside the JAO and Chancery buildings heard the sound of helicopters and began to smile with joy, saying it must be the Rescue Force. The deputy chief of mission reportedly said that *"When I saw the words 'MARINES' on the sides of those large helicopters, I knew we were safe"*. The Rescue Force arrived just in time as the walls around the US Compound were being scaled by the African Rebel Forces. The arrival of the two helicopters and the presence of the 60-man Rescue Force stopped the attack. The rebel forces retreated back across the street leaving some ladders on the Compound walls.

It was approximately 0710 hrs when the Super Stallion helicopters touched down in the US Compound. On landing, the nine Navy Seals lead by Commander Stephen R. Luoma, quickly exited the helicopters running in a vee formation toward the Chancery building to concentrate on protecting US Ambassador James K. Bishop and augmenting the US Embassy five Marine security guards (MSGs).

As the Marines came out of the Super Stallion helicopters to form a 360° defensive perimeter around the landing zone, men, women and children began coming out of the rear of the JAO and Chancery buildings clapping and cheering. The weather was sunny and hot. Most of them had on casual clothing, but there were a few women with dresses on and several men were wearing suits. Within the crowd, we could see that there was a mixture of different nationalities. They quickly went back into the buildings for protection so that no one would be hit by flying bullets. Our arrival gave them comfort and the feeling of protection. Their minds and emotions were now relaxed and at ease. We were then met by one of the Marine security guards carrying his MP-5 sub-machine gun who said *"We are so glad to see you guys"*. He then asked where our commander was. We pointed him to our battalion commander, Lieutenant Colonel McAleer. When he reached the Marine Commander, he pointed out where the African Rebel Forces held their positions and also pointed out the best positions to deploy the Rescue Force. The two Marine Platoons from Charlie Company under the leadership of Lieutenant Colonel Robert P. McAleer would work with the Embassy security officer and the 30 Somali contract guards to set up a defensive perimeter around the Compound wall to defend the US Embassy and protect subsequent evacuations. We moved out from the helicopter landing zone and immediately began to secure the Compound, deploying along the walls and on the roof tops of the Embassy buildings. We knocked down the assault ladders that the African Rebel Forces had been using to scale the walls only moments before.

The two-man sniper team found the perfect position on the top of the water tower where they had an overall view of the rebels' positions and the city at large. From our positions, you could see the African Rebel Forces moving in the early morning shadows, carrying their AK-47 assault rifles and rocket-propelled grenades (RPGs). We could hear the crackling of machine gun fire and explosions throughout the city.

Charlie Company Commander Captain Dysart and 2nd and 3rd Platoon commanders talked with Lieutenant Colonel McAleer about the defense of the US Embassy and quickly realized that there were not enough Marines to cover the entire perimeter. Second Platoon covered the northern and western walls, and the 3rd Platoon covered the southern area of the Compound. Dragon anti-tank teams were set up across from both gates (on the northern and western walls). The Navy Seal team was in positions on the roof of the Chancery building where they covered most of the southeastern portion of the Compound. Shortly after the Rescue Force were in position to defend the US Embassy, a US Air Force special operations AC-130 gunship arrived overhead to gather intelligence and provide fire support which would unleash its deadly lethal weapons if needed.

On board the Air Force AC-130 specter gunship was a crew of 12 airmen, which included five officers and 7 enlisted personnel that consisted of 2 pilots, a navigator, an electronic warfare officer, a fire control officer, flight engineer, sensor operator, aerial gunners and a load master. The AC-130 specter gunship was armed with 25 mm Gatling-type cannons, 40 mm cannons and a 105 mm Howitzer. I was with Captain D. Spasojevich, the forward air control officer who made radio contact with the AC-130 gunship using the PRC 113 radio. The gunship was flying high enough where we could not see it. Just the presence of the gunship was enough to know if the US Embassy was attacked by an overwhelming force of armed insurgents. Captain Spasojevich would call in an airstrike, and the fire power alone from the monstrous AC-130 gunship would annihilate them. He took over the radio from me, and I linked back up with my fire team.

US Ambassador James K. Bishop had an initial conversation with the overall commander of the Rescue Force, Marine Lieutenant Colonel Willard D. Oats. Both men greeted each other and shook hands. Ambassador Bishop asked Lieutenant Colonel Oats what his instructions were, and he responded by saying *"My instructions are to take instructions from you"*. Ambassador Bishop's response was *"That sounds pretty good"*. Ambassador Bishop made it clear what the rules of engagement were and the use of deadly force. His specific instructions were that the Marines were not to fire unless they were directly threatened or had his authorization. Deadly force can be used if African Rebel Forces begin coming over the walls with obvious hostile intent, or if the situation deteriorates significantly. Ambassador Bishop also outlined several zones of defense: around the entire Embassy Compound; around the JAO and Chancery buildings (the two "safe-haven" buildings); the Marine house; and the helicopter landing zone. Ambassador Bishop stated that if a choice had to be made, he preferred a withdrawal to the third zone before the use of deadly force. His rationale was very clear. He wanted to avoid creating the impression that the 60-man Rescue Force was intervening in any way in the ongoing conflict in Mogadishu. He feared that any shooting might create the impression in one or more of the groups that the United States was intervening against them.

It had now been one hour since the Rescue Force arrived. The two CH-53Es Super Stallion helicopters were still on the ground preparing to load the first evacuees.

Sixty-one evacuees, including all non-official Americans in the Compound, the ambassadors from Nigeria, Turkey, the United Arab Emirates, and the Omani Charge D'Affaires, were loaded on the Super Stallions for the return flight to the USS Guam which was now some 350 miles away. Everyone was strapped in their seatbelts with their life preservers on. The two Super Stallion helicopters lifted off the ground at 0820 hrs and headed straight out to sea where they made radio contact with the third KC-130 tanker plane that would refuel them. The helicopters would fly at the altitude of 6000 feet to refuel, which would expose the evacuees to the cold air. The evacuees were given what blankets were available, and crew members volunteered some of their clothing to help keep them warm. One evacuee asked a crew member what to do with his automatic pistol (it was promptly confiscated).

When the pilots reached the third aerial refueling control point (ARCP), it was difficult for several reasons. For this evolution, there was only one KC-130 which was therefore carrying more fuel. This forced the KC-130 to fly faster to avoid a stall. The refueling, therefore, occurred at about 125 knots, rather than the preferred 110 knots. More seriously, the KC-130 drogue mal-deployed, and the aircraft developed a fuel leak. When the Super Stallion went to refuel, the pilots were confronted with a much narrower drogue, which was difficult to plug into. Major Dan Schultz's Super Stallion was forced to fly at an angle to minimize the fuel spraying on the helicopter and only took on one-half the fuel planned. Many of the evacuees had never flown in a helicopter let alone flown in one that was being refueled in air by KC-130 tanker planes. As the crew chief observed the evacuees, he noticed some of them were a little nervous, especially the children as they watched this evolution take place. The second Super Stallion took 6 or 7 passes before successfully plugging. While this was going on, Major Dan Schultz was evaluating whether to divert one or both Super Stallion helicopters to the Somali Desert if the refueling failed. At the end of the refueling, both helicopters took in enough fuel to reach the USS Guam.

The outbound refueling KC-130 tanker plane gave the two Super Stallion helicopters final navigation and headed back to Oman, over 1,100 miles away. The KC-130 continued to act as a communications relay between Guam and the two CH-53Es until out of range. The two KC-130s from the inbound refueling had remained overhead until the outbound refueling was completed. Once the third refueling operation was complete, the two inbound refueling KC-130s flew to Mombassa, Kenya, where they refueled and awaited orders to conduct another mission in support of CH-53E operations. At 1040 hrs, almost 8 hours after the initial launch, the two CH-53E Super Stallion helicopters touched down on the USS Guam where they were met by teams to handle the evacuees. The officers and crews of the USS Guam and USS Trenton had carefully prepared for the needs of the evacuees. This included establishing a medical triage station, arranging berthing for both genders, caring for children, protecting individual property, accounting for evacuees by nationality and status, and providing food and clothing, while at the same time supporting operations ashore.

All VIPs would be separated out on the flight deck and brought immediately to officers' country. The remaining evacuees would ride the elevator down from the flight deck to the hangar deck where they would be processed. A medical screening would be conducted first. The USS Guam's medical personnel had prepared for a mass casualty situation. Guam had an unusually large medical team aboard, in addition to an augmented ship's medical contingent. A large share of BSSG-4s medical personnel were aboard. The operating rooms were prepared and beds readied for casualties. The helicopter pilots were to warn the ship if there were any wounded aboard, even though the helicopters would be met by two Navy corpsmen who would ask if any persons needed medical assistance. After all 61 evacuees were out of both helicopters and clear of the flight deck, the pilots and crews of the Super Stallion helicopters would not return to Mogadishu with reinforcements, but rather flew to the USS Trenton where their role in the mission ended.

After another difficult refueling in route, the crews were exhausted from the weary flight in and out of Mogadishu and not yet capable of another demanding mission. Marine CH-46 Sea Knight helicopters stationed on board the USS Guam would carry out subsequent evacuations, once the ships brought them within range of the US Embassy. The original plan called for the two Super Stallion helicopters to bring a second echelon of Marines into the US Embassy. Lieutenant Colonel Oats believed he needed another 44 Marines to ensure security and process the evacuees efficiently and effectively. Colonel Doyle realized that Lieutenant Colonel Oats' job was difficult, but absent a concerted effort by African Rebel Forces to storm the US Embassy, he felt another high-risk insertion flight by the exhausted crews of the two Super Stallion helicopters could not be justified. The situation was very tense. The African Rebel Forces were positioned in front of the US Embassy like a pack of vultures.

Word had filtered down to the rebel forces that US Marines and Navy Seals were on board the helicopters that touched down in the US Compound. They heard about the reputation of the US Marines and Navy Seals and were hesitant about making any moves to assault the US Embassy. Soon a second group of African Rebel Forces arrived at the US Embassy, unaware of the Marines and Navy Seals inside. They quickly disembarked from their vehicles and told the US Embassy perimeter guard to open the gate or we'll blow you away, and then they looked up and saw heavily armed Marines and Seals on the rooftops of the Embassy buildings with their weapons pointed at them. They paused and then said in Somali, *"Igaralli ahow"*, which means *"Excuse me, I didn't mean it, my mistake"*. The one who seemed to be their leader motioned with his hand for them to retreat across the street with the other rebel forces where they began to collaborate, while the Marines and Seals kept them in the sights of their weapons. Meanwhile, Marines and US Embassy employees prepared for subsequent evacuations, although the shortage of staff to operate the ECC severely hindered the process.

Ambassador Bishop, Lieutenant Colonel Oats, and the other hard-pressed Americans would have to complete all tasks with the personnel on hand. US Embassy personnel provided a variety of additional support and augmentation to the 60-man Rescue Force from the ships. There were five permanently stationed Marine security guards (MSGs), a number of Embassy security personnel, and the 30 Somali contract guards who were an important component of the defense of the Compound. To guarantee common communication, the Embassy security officer supplied many of the Marine officers and non-commissioned officers with Motorola hand-held radios that the US Embassy used for security communication. Even with the additional US Embassy security personnel, the perimeter defense of the Compound was still thin. Lieutenant Colonel Oats did not want to weaken the perimeter defense by using Lieutenant Colonel McAleer's Marines in the ECC, but felt that eventually it would be necessary to do so.

Several Marines that were doused with fuel on the Super Stallion helicopter that I was riding (including my team member Lance Corporal Dennis) took quick 3-minute showers at the Marine House to wash the fuel off their bodies and their desert-camouflaged fatigues. They used washcloths soaked in soapy water to hand wash the areas of their desert fatigues that were covered with JP-5 fuel. When Lance Corporal Dennis linked back up with our fire-team, he showed us where the JP-5 fuel actually removed some of his skin after he showered. The JP-5 fuel was very potent. Fortunately for the rest of my team, we escaped large dousing of the fuel. We were currently set in a defensive position near Gate 1. Afterwards, my team moved out on foot and began patrolling inside the US Compound. I moved my team out in a wedge formation, and I positioned myself on the left flank of the team. We patrolled the west end of the Compound looking for any armed Somalians trying to infiltrate the US Embassy Compound. The Compound was very large and there were a lot of open areas where armed Somalians could come through. We patrolled in silence, and when we reached the Compound's western wall, we turned around and headed back towards Gate 1. We were prepared to engage any armed Somalian intruder with deadly force. For right now, it seemed that the main threat was at Gate 1 where 250 armed African Rebel Forces were positioned across the street. The Embassy was receiving harassing fire and you could hear the rounds impacting on the Compound walls. There were even times where we had to take cover. My squad leader Sergeant J.D. Jennings who was detached out from 2nd Platoon as a sniper for the rescue mission and the spotter Sergeant Wells who was a former Marine Corp sniper instructor, were in position on the US Embassy water tower, which at 102 feet was the tallest structure in the Compound and provided good views in all directions.

After the two-man sniper team was in position a little over an hour, a Somalian about 400 to 500 meters away began to fire at them. Sergeant J.D. Jennings had the Somalian in the crosshairs of the scope on his M40 sniper rifle that shoots a 7.62 mm round. Sergeant Wells, using the hand-held Motorola radio, called Lieutenant Colonel McAleer requesting permission to take out the lone Somalian who was firing at them. Lieutenant Colonel McAleer denied the request and ordered the sniper team to come down from the water tower. Marines and Navy Seals' trigger-fingers were itching, and we were eager to return fire, but Ambassador Bishop asserted his authority and refused to allow the Marines and Navy Seals to return fire unless absolutely necessary. His goal was to evacuate the US Embassy without a single incident or shot being fired. Throughout the day, foreign diplomats and individuals desiring to be evacuated with the US rescue operation contacted the US Embassy. The consistent response was that foreign nationals were welcome, but they had to make their own way to the US Embassy Compound.

The Rescue Force reacted to a new situation – a major challenge to rescue 22 people who were trapped at the office of military cooperation. The 22 people included Colonel David Stanley, the chief of the office; other Americans; one Filipino; and a badly abused Kenyan Ambassador, his wife and staff. Marine commanders and the Navy Seal team commander sent three Marines and six Navy Seals to augment Embassy security in three bullet-proof hardened commercial Embassy vehicles to proceed to that location immediately. Corporal B.J. Pettit from my squad was one of the three Marines going out. Although the OMC Compound was only a quarter-mile away from the US Embassy, there was the possibility of running into a roadblock where there might be demands for vehicles to be surrendered. Ambassador Bishop ordered the convoy not to stop and to shoot its way through if necessary.

At 0847 hrs, the three bullet-proof vehicles left the US Embassy. As the convoy rode through the streets of Mogadishu to the objective, the Marines and Seals observed carefully for rebel forces. The city was like the Wild, Wild West. The three vehicle's windows were tinted. Corporal B.J. Pettit observed seeing men, women and children of all ages looting everything in sight. Many Somalians were armed with weapons, and they were carrying pistols, rifles, automatic weapons and RPGs. There were no law enforcement officers to enforce any laws or regulations. It was every man, woman and child for themselves. It was complete survival. It was very sad to see how a bloody civil war destroyed a city. There were even some Somalian women scrounging for food while carrying their babies on their backs in this dangerous environment. As the rescue convoy proceeded to the Office of Military Cooperation, the three bullet-proof US Embassy vehicles received a lot of stares from armed Somalians. The three Marines and six Navy Seals were prepared to shoot their way through any roadblocks. Corporal B.J. Pettit was prepared to 'rock and roll'. He had his M203 rifle with grenade launcher on burst. When the rescue convoy arrived at the OMC Compound, four Americans, one Filipino and seventeen Kenyans were waiting in lightly armored vehicles. The two mini-convoys emerged and sped back to the US Embassy, as the Embassy lookouts contacted the convoy by radio informing them of the absence of Somali military traffic on Afgoy Road outside the gate, and that they were clear. Within ten minutes, the mini-convoy was safely inside the US Compound.

After the recovery of the group at the OMC Compound, the US Embassy focused on what help they could provide to other diplomatic missions that were trapped at their Embassies. An issue arose with the Soviet Embassy personnel. The Soviets had made contact with the US Embassy by radio the previous day, informing them that they had been attacked and lost vehicles to armed looters the day before. The Soviet Ambassador, Vladimir Korneev, did not feel that he and his staff could safely make their way to the US Embassy Compound without assistance. Ambassador Bishop agreed to escort them with permanent US Embassy security personnel. To augment this force, he contracted the Somali police under a Major Sayed who agreed to support the effort for a fee. The rescue convoy comprised of permanent Embassy security personnel, and Somali police departed the US Embassy at 1130 hrs. An hour later, the convoy safely arrived back at the US Embassy with 39 Soviet guests who would be evacuated with the US rescue operation. Ambassador Bishop used a similar approach in rescuing 15 British nationals from their Embassy, which was in a more dangerous area. They also arrived safely at the US Embassy, but the British Ambassador and German Charge were trapped in a building across from the President's headquarters where they had been under intense fire for five days. Special arrangements made with a senior Somali resulted in the rescue and recovery of both brave men. They joyfully reunited with their staff already at the US Embassy. An arrangement to escort the South Koreans from their Embassy unfortunately was unsuccessful, because they did not trust the Somali guards sent from the US Embassy. They feared the Somalian guards were armed rebel forces that would take them hostage for ransom and possibly kill them. They chose not to come with the Somalian guards which could result in tragic consequences for them. No other attempt was made from the US Embassy to rescue the South Koreans from their Embassy. They were on their own. At this point, every American and foreign national that were going to be evacuated with the US military rescue operation were now safely inside the US Embassy Compound. The understaffed ECC, established by Marine Officer Major William N. Saunders on the US Embassy grounds, worked hard to identify and process evacuees under difficult circumstances.

Lieutenant Colonel Oats utilized members of the US Embassy staff and reluctantly pulled some of Lieutenant Colonel McAleer's Marines from their defensive positions to assist Major Saunders in the ECC, to provide security, administrative help, checking identities, screening potential evacuees, creating manifests and accounting for authorized evacuees. US Embassy secretaries remained at their word processors, supporting ECC operations throughout the day, with combat-ready Marines wandering by their desks.

One difficulty encountered almost immediately, which remained a problem throughout the operation for the Rescue Force, was the presence of a large number of Somali nationals in the Compound, who were primarily foreign service nationals (FSNs), and who worked for the US Embassy including the 30 Somali contract guards. The Somalis located throughout the Compound created a rather confusing security picture. Many of the Somali FSNs wished to be evacuated, but Ambassador Bishop explained to them that international law forbids evacuation of natives. In addition, the Ambassador explained that he risked creating the impression of interference in the Somali Civil War if Somali nationals were evacuated as well. Dealing with Somalis who wished to be evacuated was a constant issue. During processing in the JAO Building, further winnowing occurred and many Somalis were turned away there.

In the afternoon, President Siad Barre's brother, who was a Major General and Chief of Police, requested to be evacuated along with 25 members of his family. After a loud confrontation, Ambassador Bishop had Lieutenant Colonel Oats escort the Major General (who was drunk) out of the Compound. Because of the mounting pressure and collapse of the Somalian government from the bloody civil war, the Somalian chief of police drank alcohol heavily that morning until afternoon before showing up at the US Embassy. He was hoping that he and 25 members of his family who were still in the city of Mogadishu would be evacuated with the US rescue operation. He, along with many Somalian military soldiers, law enforcement officials and government leaders did not know what the future held for them. During a break in the firing around the US Embassy, Ambassador Bishop met with the FSNs under a tree, inside the Compound to talk with them. Although they had remained loyal, the US Embassy did not have enough cash to pay all their wages due because the banks had closed down. Ambassador Bishop explained to the FSNs that the Embassy would leave what cash they could and the Commissary keys with the FSN committee to distribute money and food among them. The Ambassador also promised that everything possible would be done to send funds to them from Nairobi, Kenya.

Leaving the FSNs behind would be an extremely painful experience for many, such as personnel officer Sharon Nichols, Bill Mueller, and Walt Fleming, who had particularly strong bonds with the FSNs who worked directly for them. Everyone was troubled leaving their household help, especially after Mike Shanklin's manservant turned up brutally beaten by armed looters. This was a very sad moment for Ambassador Bishop, and he felt very badly about leaving them in these circumstances. The US Embassy had welcomed their families into the Compound to protect them, but obviously with the departure of the US Rescue Force and authorized evacuees nearing, their protection would soon be gone. Though they faced an uncertain future, the Somalis accepted their fate and would remain on their jobs to the end. At this point, only a handful made futile requests to be evacuated.

Meanwhile, the USS Guam and USS Trenton were still steaming south at flank speed towards Mogadishu. It would be hours before the two-ship task force would arrive off the coast of Mogadishu with Marine reinforcements and to evacuate the US Embassy. The African Rebel Forces were still formed outside the Embassy Compound walls with their AK-47 assault rifles, rocket-propelled grenades and ladders. We knew that the rebel forces were not going anywhere because the US Embassy was the grand prize that they wanted. The Marines and Navy Seals' presence on the Embassy rooftops and in defensive positions around the perimeter of the Compound showed the rebel forces that the US Embassy was not ready for new management. There was still sporadic fire around the Embassy where some rounds flew over the Embassy Compound or hit Embassy Buildings, including a rocket-propelled grenade round that hit the Compounds southern wall in the afternoon.

So far, the fire discipline of the Rescue Force had been excellent; we had not fired one shot. All it would take for the situation to turn deadly was if the African Rebel Forces became bold enough to attack the US Embassy. They would remain under our watchful eyes until the mission was complete and we were extracted. Many of the Marines and Navy Seals had freshly cooked food brought to their fighting positions from US Embassy staff. My fire-team was in a defensive position on the far western end of the Compound, so we did not receive any of the home-cooked meals from the US Embassy staff. But Sergeant Hendrix's 3rd Squad from our Platoon did receive freshly cooked meals from the Embassy staff. They thanked the Embassy staff with big smiles on their faces as well as complimenting them on how delicious the food was. This was a welcome substitute for meals ready to eat (MREs). US Embassy staff personnel Karen Aguilar offered one Navy Seal a plateful of Rock Cornish Game Hen. He told her he'd rather not *"go into combat with a baby chicken in my stomach"*. Karen Aguilar recalled when the Rescue Force arrived. She described that it was sudden and frightening, even for the diplomats they sought to rescue. Karen stated that each man must have been carrying 200 pounds of equipment, they looked about seven feet tall, and on every inch of their bodies they had this terrible paint. *"They looked ugly; they looked mean; they looked like swamp creatures."*

The nine Navy Seals wore their green-camouflaged fatigues and camouflaged their faces with paint. The Marines wore their desert-camouflaged fatigues. Since the Rescue Force went in heavily armed, we looked three times our normal size which made us look like giants to those we came to rescue. Ambassador Bishop authorized the Rescue Force to take whatever they wished from the Embassy. While the hundreds of cases of alcohol and beer beckoned, this mostly meant sodas, candy bars and T-shirts as souvenirs. The Ambassador also Okayed any other "plundering" of the Embassy for equipment, such as Xerox machines and computers that might be useful on board the Guam and Trenton, rather than leaving them behind for rebel forces and looters. We did not plunder any of the equipment or take any of the alcohol. Our mission was to rescue innocent people and get them out of harm's way.

It was now early evening and the Rescue Force forward air controller (FAC) Captain Spagojevich began preparation of the helicopter landing zone (HLZ). Several cars were parked in the HLZ, many of which were without keys. They were broken into and pushed out of the HLZ. The evacuation of the US Embassy would be conducted at night with the Compound completely darkened, with Marine helicopter pilots and the Rescue Force on the ground using night-vision devices. The 60-man Rescue Force had gone in heavily equipped with night-vision devices. With nightfall quickly approaching and the darkening of the US Embassy, Marines and Navy Seals equipped with night-vision devices would be able to see any potential threat well before that threat could see them. Marine CH-46 pilots flying with night-vision goggles (NVGs) would be able to fly their helicopters totally darkened into a dark landing zone. Potential threat forces would practically be unable to see the helicopters. The use of night-vision devices would give US forces a major edge over Somali forces (government, rebel and criminal) that were a threat to the US Embassy.

Teams of Marines continued to prepare the HLZ. An infrared strobe was placed on the Embassy tower, and chemical lights were dug into the helicopter landing zone in a NATOY and used to mark the light poles that surrounded the HLZ. Because there was no central light switch in the US Embassy Compound, Marines had to move from building to building to turn off the lights, and some of the outside lights could be extinguished only by cutting the power supply. This continued until late in the evening. The lights on the Marine House were the last building to be extinguished, which was done by the cables being cut. As the night quickly came upon us, the Compound was pitch-dark with the only light coming from the moon. Using our night-vision goggles, we had good observation of the rebels' movement. They were still positioned outside the Embassy Gate 1 like a pack of vultures. You could hear them talking, and it seemed like they were getting a little anxious. We kept a close visual on their movements.

Word came down that the USS Guam and USS Trenton had arrived on station, and the ships were positioned 30 miles off the coast. The evacuation of the US Embassy would commence at 2330 hrs. There would be a total of four waves of CH-46 helicopters from HMM-263 and HMM-365 with five helicopters landing in the HLZ on each wave. The first three waves would evacuate the Americans and foreign nationals, and the last wave would extract the Rescue Force. As the evacuees were being prepared for evacuation, a couple of issues arose. Evacuees were told they could bring one bag of luggage a piece; more than one evacuee attempted to bring more than that. Marines who were pulled from the perimeter defense had to enforce the rule. My fire-team remained outside in a defensive position. Several of the evacuees had pets they wished to bring with them. This, however, was not permitted, and Marines had to enforce this rule as well. Most pets were killed by their owners using poison. None of the evacuees caused any problems, they complied with the rules. The extra luggage was placed in an open area of the JAO Building, and the pets that were poisoned were carried and placed in an isolated area outside. After all issues were enforced and resolved, the US Embassy and ECC made final preparations to evacuate the Embassy.

On board the USS Guam, the CH-46 Marine pilots received their final briefing and intelligence update. The pilots boarded their helicopters and put on their night-vision goggles. They went through a series of checks with their night-vision goggles to ensure they were properly functioning. By 2300 hrs, five sticks of 15 evacuees were being set up outside the Embassy JAO Building facing the helicopter landing zone. The evacuees were organized into three waves. All the evacuees in the first two waves were from the JAO Building. The third wave consisted of US Embassy personnel (including Ambassador Bishop) still working in the Chancery Building.

Once again the perimeter defense of the Compound was weakened even more because Marines had to be pulled (which included me) to protect and assist evacuees to the helicopters and to ensure no Somali FSNs attempted to rush the helicopters. By 2330 hrs, the US Embassy Compound was ready for the CH-46 evacuation to commence, but would be delayed an hour because the Air Force AC-130 gunship that would cover the evacuation by providing fire support and intelligence would not arrive on station until after midnight. This delay was not good, with the US Embassy being threatened by three different groups of Somalians (government, rebel and criminal). As the Marines on the perimeter defense observed the African rebels' movement through their night-vision goggles, it seemed that their curiosity was growing with the US Compound being pitch-dark. They could possibly make an attempt to assault the US Embassy at any moment, but they would definitely be met by a hail of accurate gunfire by the Marines and Navy Seals.

It was now a few minutes past midnight on January 6. The Marine CH-46 pilots on board the Guam awaiting in their helicopters received the green light to commence the evacuation of the US Embassy. The Rescue Force on the ground received word by radio to prepare for evacuation. The evacuees began coming out from the JAO Building by their country, towards the helicopter landing zone. They were organized into five sticks of 15 evacuees each stick, which included men, women and children. The Marines that were pulled from the perimeter defense to assist lined up in front of them. A Marine Warrant Officer along with my Company Commander, Captain Dysart, handed us the manifest rosters with each evacuee's name on them, so that we could verify each person. My Company Commander and the Warrant Officer proceeded back to the JAO Building. Each Marine who was lined up in front of the evacuees was assigned two sticks. I was assigned an American and Soviet Union stick. When I looked at the manifest roster for the Soviet Union, I was not even going to attempt to pronounce their names. So I asked out loud, *"Do anybody speak English?"* This beautiful Russian female came forward and said, *"I do"* with that Russian accent.

We walked down the line verifying each person. We came to a very tall man with blonde hair and a distinguished look. At that time, I did not realize he was the Russian Ambassador. After I finished verifying the Russians, I proceeded to the American stick. I went down the line verifying each name. When I came to the last person in line who was a man, his name was not on the manifest roster. He was not an American, but was a Somalian. I asked him if his name was supposed to be on the manifest roster, and he said, *"It should be, I will go back inside the Embassy Building and check".* He walked away very sad, and the Americans looking on looked sad as well. I never saw him again. I briefly talked with the Americans in the stick who said he was a Somalian who worked for the US Embassy and was very well liked, and that he was afraid to be left behind. I felt sorry for him, but I had to obey orders. Anyone whose name was not on the manifest roster was not allowed to get on the helicopters. By this time, everyone's name had been verified on the manifest rosters.

The first wave of CH-46 helicopters was en route to the US Embassy. While en route to the US Embassy, the CH-46 helicopters and the Air Force AC-130 gunship, covering the evacuation radar warning receivers, lit up as a SA-2 radar went active. The crew of the AC-130 gunship detected a kind of radar of the type associated with a Soviet-built SA-2 surface-to-air missile site tracking their aircraft. The presence of SA-2 missiles confirmed the commanders on board the USS Guam's concerns, in the beginning phases of planning the rescue operation, about the possibility of sophisticated weapons in Somalia. The SA-2 missiles posed a definite threat to the AC-130 gunship. The gunship was moved over the ocean as a result. Colonel Doyle had not been concerned for the CH-46 helicopters because he believed they would fly too low to be tracked by its radars.

The SA-2 missiles have almost no capabilities against low-altitude targets, and the CH-46 helicopters were flying at an altitude of 150 feet. The US Embassy was almost a mile inland from the ocean. You could see the ocean from the Embassy. As the five CH-46 helicopters from Marine Squadron HMM-263 approached the US Embassy, you could hear them but could not see them. As the helicopters got closer, the thump of the rotor blades got louder. Under the cover of darkness, the first wave of helicopters touched down in the US Compound in a staggered formation. Because the Compound was pitch-dark and the helicopters were totally blacked out, the helicopters were practically unseen until they were already on the ground, and then only dimly. The evacuees watched in awe. The Marines assigned to the sticks quickly moved the first wave of evacuees to their designated helicopters. I took the Soviet Union stick out first. After we got all 75 evacuees on the helicopters in the first wave, we moved back to the second wave of evacuees. The helicopter crew chiefs spent several minutes putting life preservers on the evacuees. After 20 minutes on the ground, the five CH-46 helicopters took off with the first 75 evacuees aboard.

As the first wave was taking off from the US Embassy simultaneously, the second wave of five CH-46 helicopters from Marine Squadron HMM-365 was lifting off from the USS Guam. After 12 minutes from lifting off the Guam, the second wave was touching down in the US Embassy Compound at the same time the first wave was touching down on the deck of the USS Guam. The evacuation was going smoothly and like clockwork until Somali Officer Major Sayed, who had earlier assisted in the transportation of foreign consular personnel into the US Embassy in return for cash, suddenly arrived at the gate of the US Embassy with two trucks full of soldiers demanding to speak to the Ambassador. Major Sayed had a hand grenade in one hand and a radio in the other. Speaking in a loud voice, he told the US Embassy gate guard, *"I demand that this evacuation and illegal operation cease immediately. My government has not granted the United States permission to mount such an operation".* But his government had ceased to function sometime earlier. He then threatened to shoot down any helicopters that attempted to take off. The Embassy gate guard had Ambassador Bishop on the radio. Ambassador Bishop gave instructions to have Major Sayed escorted in to meet with him. The Embassy gate guard told the Somali officer that Ambassador Bishop would like to meet with him. The head of the Embassy security detachment escorted Major Sayed into the US Compound to meet with Bishop.

The Marines on the perimeter defense were now keeping a high visibility on the Somali soldiers on the trucks as well as the rebel forces. The helicopter landing zone was positioned to the rear of the US Compound. The Somalian forces threatening the US Embassy could only hear the CH-46 helicopters flying in and out of the Compound, but could not see them. Ambassador Bishop, after conferring with Lieutenant Colonel Oats, ordered the evacuation to continue as he would begin to negotiate with Major Sayed. The Marines took the second wave of 75 evacuees and put them on their designated helicopters. Once all evacuees had their life preservers on, the second wave lifted off from the US Compound as the third wave lifted off from the USS Guam. Meanwhile as the third wave was inbound to the US Embassy, Ambassador Bishop began an interesting discussion with Major Sayed which started off with his demand that the evacuation end, which obviously the Ambassador was not going to comply with. He then ran through his request that the US Embassy evacuate him and his family, which Ambassador Bishop responded that he would take it up with the officers on the ship once he reached the ships himself. For the next three quarters of an hour, Ambassador Bishop kept Major Sayed engaged in sometimes insane conversations, while his security team remained with him, and several Navy Seals beyond the circle of light kept Sayed, his radio, and hand grenade in their sights.

Ambassador Bishop ultimately persuaded the Somali officer not to interfere. Bishop accomplished this through skillful negotiation, the help of several thousand dollars, and the keys to a US Embassy automobile of Major Sayed's choice. In the process, Ambassador Bishop managed to take possession of Sayed's radio to prevent him from calling anti-aircraft fire on the departing helicopters. If for some reason Sayed was not willing to negotiate and attempted to get on his radio, or pull the pin and clip on his grenade, or signal his soldiers in the two trucks, the situation most likely would have turned deadly. With an elite group of Marines and Navy Seals in the US Compound, the Somalian Major would not have made it out of there, and his soldiers on the trucks would not have made it into the Compound.

Thanks to the professionalism of Ambassador Bishop, he was able to diffuse a tense situation that could have turned deadly. I could only imagine if Ambassador Bishop had already departed and Major Sayed showed up with just the Rescue Force there, no doubt the outcome probably would have turned deadly. This incident created some confusion in the last evacuation waves, because Ambassador Bishop insisted on remaining in the US Compound so as to be available to handle such problems through the end of the evacuation. Bishop and his security team had been scheduled to depart in the third wave, but his decision to remain to the end meant that only four helicopters on the third wave were full, and departed as planned. The fifth helicopter remained on the ground until the arrival of the fourth wave. When the Rescue Force received word that the fourth and final wave was inbound to extract us, the Marines and several Seals that were still in defensive positions began to withdraw from the Embassy rooftops and their positions.

As the Rescue Force pulled back from the perimeter to the helicopter landing zone, they covered each other's movements while closely watching the hostile forces positioned just outside the US Compound walls. The rebel forces could see our shadows in the dark pulling back, and they knew we were leaving. This was their cue to assault the US Embassy. You could see hundreds of them inching forward with their AK-47 assault rifles, rocket-propelled grenades and ladders. The fourth wave touched down in the US Embassy Compound on schedule. Ambassador Bishop walked with Major Sayed toward the helicopter landing zone, keeping him engaged in conversation until the very last moment, to ensure that he would not have an opportunity to interfere with the evacuation's last wave. The Rescue Force quickly began to pile into the helicopters. The Navy Seals who were protecting US Ambassador James Bishop boarded helicopters when he did.

Since Ambassador Bishop and the Embassy security team did not leave on the third wave, the boarding of helicopters in the final wave did not move as smoothly as the previous three waves. The confusion caused inaccuracies in the serial manifests and the helicopter loading plan. Some Marines were sent running from helicopter to helicopter looking for seating, which complicated attempts to account for all personnel. Several times, all personnel were reported accounted for, and the helicopters were about to lift off when one CH-46 crew chief reported two marines near the HLZ. With no perimeter defense, we were very vulnerable sitting in the LZ. The two radio operators had not realized that this was the final wave, and had remained intent on maintaining communications. The crew chief ran over to them, helped them stow their equipment, and got them aboard.

The Somalian Foreign Service Nationals never attempted to rush the helicopters. They watched sadly with their families, and some were crying as the last US Marine CH-46 Sea Knight helicopters lifted off from the US Embassy Compound heading back to the sea. They knew that the African Rebel Forces would soon storm the US Embassy. I felt sad for the FSNs left behind, and I thought about the Somalian worker that I had to turn back from getting on the helicopter. At this point as I sat in the helicopter as we headed back to the ship, all I could do was think if the FSNs left behind would survive, be tortured or killed. I prayed that they would survive.

As soon as the last wave lifted off, Marine pilots could see African Rebel Forces through their night-vision goggles coming over the US Embassy Compound walls like ants. They blew down the US Embassy gate with a rocket-propelled grenade round. At 0320 hrs well before sunrise on 6 January 1991, the last wave of CH-46 Sea Knight helicopters set down on the flight deck of the USS Guam. The Rescue Force disembarked from the helicopters, and the Navy flight-deck crewmen put us on the large flight-deck elevator which lowered the 51 Marines down to the hangar bay. The nine Navy Seals secretly disappeared. When we arrived on the hangar bay, there were several foreign ambassadors and some evacuees standing there who were so grateful for us rescuing them, that they waited for us to arrive. As the Rescue Force walked off the elevator, they were clapping, cheering and shaking our hands. This brought a great feeling over me as a Marine to be a member of a 60-man Rescue Force sent on a drastic rescue mission in hostile territory to rescue men, women and children. If we had not arrived, their chances of survival would not have been good. The Rescue Force launched from the USS Guam at night on 5 January. In just a little over 24 hours later, we arrived back on the Guam at night after a successful mission. All evacuees and Rescue Force members were accounted for.

Twenty minutes after the Rescue Force arrived on the Guam, Ambassador James K. Bishop declared the evacuation complete at 0343 hrs. In all, 281 men, women and children from over 30 different nations were rescued from a bloody civil war. This included 39 Soviet citizens, 12 heads of diplomatic missions, eight ambassadors and four Charges d'affaires. The eight ambassadors were the Ambassador of the United States, Soviet Union, Great Britain, United Arab Emirates, Kenya, Nigeria, Turkey and Sudan. The four charges d'affaires were heads of the Embassy of Oman, Kuwait, Qatar and Germany. The Rescue Mission that was rapidly planned on a short notice that involved the US Navy, Marines and Air Force and was conducted as US troops prepared for war with Iraq, ended in a successful conclusion. The high-risk Rescue Mission was accomplished without loss of life or equipment.

EASTERN EXIT US EVACUEES

Category	Men	Women	Children	Total
US Govt. Employees	18	8	0	26
Military assigned to Embassy	3	0	0	3
Dependents	0	1	0	1
Private Citizens	10	10	11	31

EASTERN EXIT EVACUEES BY COUNTRY

Country	Men	Women	Children	Total
Belgium	1	0	0	1
Canada	0	1	0	1
Colombia	1	0	0	1
Denmark	5	1	0	6
Ethiopia	1	0	0	1
France	2	0	0	2
Germany	11	7	8	26
Ghana	1	0	0	1
India	4	2	0	6
Italy	15	0	0	15
Kenya	10	3	4	17
Kuwait	1	3	3	7
Liberia	1	0	0	1
Netherlands	1	0	0	1
Nigeria	5	0	0	5
Norway	1	0	0	1
Oman	2	0	0	2
Pakistan	0	1	0	1
Philippines	2	0	0	2
Portugal	2	0	0	2
Qatar	1	0	0	1
Somalia	8	14	3	25

Sri Lanka	0	1	0	1
Sudan	17	6	3	26
Sweden	1	0	0	1
Tanzania	0	1	0	1
Thailand	1	0	0	1
Turkey	5	0	10	5
UAE	2	0	0	2
U K	10	3	4	17
U S	31	19	11	61
USSR	22	16	1	39
Total	162	82	37	281

Corporal LaLand on the hangar deck of the U.S.S Guam with U.S Embassy personnel that he was protecting and putting on the helicopters in the early morning hours.

UNITED STATES SHIP GUAM (LPH 9)

On behalf of myself and the undersigned heads of diplomatic missions to Somalia, I wish to express our profound and heartfelt gratitude to the sailors and marines of USS GUAM and her embarked units for their daring, swift, gallant and humanitarian rescue of the two hundred eighty-one souls in the American Embassy Mogadishu compound, in our most desperate hours, January five and six, nineteen hundred and ninety one.

JAMES K. BISHOP
AMBASSADOR,
EMBASSY OF THE UNITED STATES OF AMERICA

VLADIMIR KORNEEV
AMBASSADOR,
EMBASSY OF THE SOVIET UNION

JOHN P. SIPARO
AMBASSADOR,
EMBASSY OF KENYA

IAN MCCLUNEY
AMBASSADOR,
EMBASSY OF GREAT BRITAIN

AL KHAGAH A'HADI
AMBASSADOR,
EMBASSY OF THE UNITED ARAB EMIRATES

MUSTAFA HASSAN AHMED
AMBASSADOR,
EMBASSY OF SUDAN

DARIRU ABUBAKAR
AMBASSADOR,
EMBASSY OF NIGERIA

HIKMET SENGENC
AMBASSADOR,
EMBASSY OF TURKEY

SAIF ALI SULTAN ALKALBANI
CHARGE D'AFFAIRES,
EMBASSY OF OMAN

MATTAR T. AL SALMA
CHARGE D'AFFAIRES
EMBASSY OF KUWAI'

SAED ABDULLA AL-MANSOURI
CHARGE D'AFFAIRES,
EMBASSY OF QATAR

HANS-JUERGEN K'
CHARGE D'A
EMBASSY O

(11)h

Chapter 8

After The Mission

Almost as soon as the last wave of CH-46 Sea Knight helicopters landed on the Guam, the two ships headed north toward Muscat, Oman where the evacuees would be off-loaded. Initially, the two ships were to head to Mombasa, Kenya, and the evacuees would only spend 24 to 36 hours aboard ship. But Guam and Trenton received orders to take the evacuees to Muscat, Oman instead. As a result, the evacuees would spend five to six days aboard ship. The large number of foreign civilians that would reside aboard Guam and Trenton for this length of time created a complicated situation for forces preparing to go to war.

On arrival aboard ship, the evacuees were processed first and then later moved to sleeping quarters. Processing included separating VIPs from other evacuees, providing medical treatment, searching evacuees and their luggage, and verifying evacuees' identities and nationalities. Over 125 Marines and Sailors were present on the hangar bay to help with processing – from the Chaplain greeting evacuees to "baggage handlers" and Navy medical personnel standing by to render medical assistance. There were a number of people who needed medical assistance; the most serious were two wounded individuals: an American woman who had been shot in the abdomen two days earlier and went into surgery on the Guam, and a man who had been beaten and stabbed.

Both were treated by the USS Guam medical staff, and they were recovering and doing well.

The first step in processing was each evacuee's belongings were searched. The evacuees stepped onto a pallet where ship security used a metal detector to search for weaponry. No weapons were found. The only contraband detected was some alcohol which was thrown overboard. The evacuees were then asked to fill out forms, providing basic medical information and identification information. A number of Somalis who had gotten into the evacuation process were worried about being returned from the ships to Somalia. These evacuees lied about their nationality until they felt secure that they would not be flown back into Mogadishu. It was initially estimated that processing would take about four hours for each evacuee, but it actually took half as long.

After completing processing, evacuees were escorted to their sleeping quarters. The US Embassy's senior staff and Chiefs of Diplomatic Missions were taken to Guam's officer's quarters. The Rescue Force had been up for over 24 hours without any sleep. After we turned our ammunition in and locked away our weapons and equipment, we hit the sack and were allowed to sleep in late. Corporal Jenkins, Corporal Pettit and I woke up about 1030 hrs, showered and went together to lunch at 1100 hrs. After we ate lunch, our Platoon had a debriefing with our Platoon Commander, 2nd Lieutenant H.R. VanOpdorp, at 1200 hrs. During our debriefing, we were informed that the African Rebel Forces that came over the walls of the US Embassy used rocket-propelled grenades to blast open Embassy doors. They shot an RPG round through a warehouse door, and the shell hit the alcohol inside and everything burned down. According to other reports from

Mogadishu corroborated by amateur snapshots, the armed rebels gained entry to the Chancery Building and took everything of value that they could find. When they came to the inner vault (where the diplomats, their staffs and families planned to hide if the US Rescue Force did not arrive in time), the Rebel Forces destroyed it with rocket-propelled grenades. These photographs showed nothing except blackened rubble where the evacuees would have been. The Rebel Forces looted and destroyed everything in sight. We also were informed that the armed rebels killed several Somali Embassy workers. I wondered if the Somali worker I had turned back because he was not on the manifest roster was one of the Somalians killed. It bothered me, but I had to obey my orders.

After our debriefing was finished, our Platoon went to the hangar bay of the ship where we had the opportunity to meet the evacuees. Steps were taken on the Guam to allow the evacuees some privacy, as well as to create situations where the crews and embarked Marines would meet them. An area of the hangar deck was assigned as a social area. Over 200 Sailors and Marines aboard Guam volunteered on top of their normal duty to be guides for evacuees (no evacuees were allowed to wander outside their berthing areas without a guide). By the direction of Guam's Commanding Officer Captain Saffell, the evacuees were called "guests of the United States" to help create a warm atmosphere. The USS Guam's Sailors and Marines rolled out the red carpet for our 281 guests, offering them warmth, food, clothing and a friendly voice. Every rack for each guest aboard "Hotel" Guam had a fresh change of sheets with a Hershey's Chocolate Kiss on the pillow. There was a Sailor dressed as a clown on the hangar bay to entertain the children. The kids could not stop smiling and laughing. They were having such a good time. Several Marines helped bottle-feed four-week-old Mary Lynda Rugh, the Somali infant that US Embassy staff workers Mike and Karen were bringing home to adopt much sooner than planned.

My fellow Platoon brothers and I met many of the guests, and they were shaking our hands and thanking us. I personally met and took pictures with some of the Americans that I was assigned to safely put on the helicopters, and it was a great time of fellowship. There were a few challenges that the Guam encountered while the guests were aboard. One was providing communication support for the guests. The US Embassy was given a satellite link to Washington, and the flag bridge on the USS Guam was turned over to the US Ambassador. Other diplomatic missions were able to send messages as well, including perhaps the first TASS news article sent via US Navy message traffic.

Other challenges were dietary restrictions of the Islamic guests had to be respected (pork was clearly identified, and all meals had non-pork choices). The wardroom lounge was turned into a daycare center for young children. With an Amphibious Assault Ship that was preparing to go to war which is embarked with strictly all men on board, no one would have ever thought that a large number of women would come on board for an extended period of time. There were a total of 82 women whose private and personal needs had to be confronted. Senior officers of the USS Guam dealt with these issues. The number one issue was that the Guam did not have enough sanitary napkins for all of the women. The only other alternative would be to use toilet paper. The Guam's laundry room was made available for women to wash and dry their undergarments and clothes. There were over a dozen African women who had to be explained to how to use Western toilets because of their cultural differences. The Guam's Sailors and Marines worked hard to overcome all challenges to make the 281 guests from over 30 different nations feel at home. The guests were allowed to shop at the ship's store, and it was not long before all the clothing was bought out. There were several Ambassadors who were soon wearing Guam sweatshirts or attired in naval uniforms they purchased at the ship's store. Many embarked servicemen donated clothing to guests. The guests were also given leftover Christmas gifts received from organizations back in the states that provided each guest with a basic toiletry kit, and each child with many pounds of candy to satisfy their sweet tooth. At church services on Guam, some embarked service members and guests prayed together. US Embassy personnel Lynda Walker's powerful rendition of Black spirituals brought radiance to the faces of the young Marines and Sailors who joined her in song, and delight to the Soviet Ambassador who was pleased to be invited to join the fellowship. Embassy athletes were welcome when the flight deck was opened to those desiring exercise. Those that ran found themselves jogging into a 35-knot wind.

Early in the morning of 10 January, Guam's Commanding Officer Captain Saffell announced the birth of the 282nd guest. The wife of Sudanese Ambassador Mustafa Hassan Ahmed gave birth to a healthy baby boy in what might have been the first Caesarean delivery ever aboard a US Navy combatant ship. (In keeping with an old Navy tradition, the lad's name was engraved on the inside of the ship's bell.) The next day, 11 January 1991, the

USS Guam and USS Trenton arrived in Muscat, Oman to offload the guests. Due to Omani restrictions, there was no press to greet the ship and guests at the end of this operation. As the guests prepared to leave, many of them prayed silently that the servicemen remaining aboard would be spared the horrors of war, as with our help, they had escaped the chaos of Mogadishu. Before disembarking, US Ambassador James K. Bishop addressed the Sailors and Marines aboard Guam via the cable television system: *"Few of us would have been alive today if we had been outside your reach. It was only due to your extraordinary efforts that we made it. We will take a part of each of you with us the rest of our lives"*.

Subsequent events made it clear that the Marines and Seals came just in time, as armed rebels came over the US Embassy walls as the last wave of CH-46 Sea Knight helicopters were lifting off. We were very impressed by the professionalism of Eastern Exit. The Marines and Navy Seals on the ground in Mogadishu appeared at all times as masters of the situation. The best indicator of their competence was the mission's success: the rescue and evacuation of 281 people from an embattled city without death or injury to either evacuees or military personnel. The actions of those protecting the US Embassy and evacuating evacuees were indeed heroic, and the actions aboard the USS Guam were indeed compassionate.

When all 282 guests were offloaded and standing on the dock, they were waving, including the little children, saying their last good-byes and "thank-you" as the USS Guam and USS Trenton prepared to pull out of port to join the other 29 ships of the Amphibious Task Force. We were back on station in the Kuwait Theater of Operation for the final workup for Operation Desert Storm. On 17 January 1991 at 0400 hrs, the USS Guam's Commanding Officer Captain Saffell announced over the ship's P.A. system that the war had begun. US and Allied war planes were bombing Baghdad and other designated targets. US and Allied forces went from Operation Desert Shield to Operation Desert Storm, and we knew that the ground war would soon follow.

On 26 January 1991, 1st Battalion 2nd Marines flew back into the Desert of Oman for our last and final Sea Soldier IV training exercise which lasted for a few days. When Charlie Company arrived back on the USS Guam, we cleaned our weapons and gear, and continued preparing for ground Combat Operations. Each Marine in Charlie Company received one set of flex handcuffs that would be used for Iraq prisoners. There were many veteran Marines in my Platoon. But none of us had ever been in combat. We had trained for years for this moment, and we were ready to go.

On 24 February 1991 at 0400 hrs, the ground offensive began. Later that morning, we asked our commanders, *"When are we going in?"* And their response was that we have not received our mission yet. But that mission would never come. The ground war lasted only 100 hours and then the war was over. We learned that the Allied Commander-in-Chief General Norman. A. Schwarzkopf's battle plan was to use the Amphibious Task Force comprised of 31 ships from the Atlantic and Pacific fleets with elements of the 4th and 5th Marine Expeditionary Brigades and the 13th Marine Expeditionary Unit Special Operations Capable embarked on board these ships as a deception operation. Deception operations have been one that has been practiced by military strategists for centuries. It became one of the largest deceptions in military history. The USS Guam and the other ships of the ATF provided a force that checked or held in place a very large Iraqi ground force in Kuwait. In anticipation of an amphibious assault by US Marines from the ATF, five or six divisions of Iraqi forces were built up along the coastline, leaving their internal defenses weak. If those ground forces had not been tied up at the coastline, the results of the war could have been significantly different. The casualty rates could have been much higher, and many battles could have swayed in different ways. There were a lot of gung-ho Marines who were upset because we had been out there for so long, training and preparing for the war, but would not see any action, because we were part of a deception battle plan. However, a cease-fire had been declared, and we received word that we would be returning home soon.

We were very happy that we were heading back home. It had been a long time at sea. As we began to make our transit home, we made a port call in Haifa, Israel on 24 March for our fourth liberty and wash-down. This was my second time going to Israel while serving in the Marines. This time they had tours set up to see the Holy Land. I felt for a long time that God had a calling upon my life, but I just didn't know what it was. But I was definitely going to take advantage of this opportunity and sign up. Churches, Christian groups and tourists travel to the Holy Land frequently. Airfare and costs can be expensive, but there are some discounted rates. I was blessed to travel there for free. The tours they set up for us were less than $100.00.

My buddy Corporal Jenkins and I chose the tour that would make a stop at the Jordan River, where Jesus was baptized, as well as other significant sites. We were told to take our Physical training shorts because we would be able to get in the Jordan River. Everyone taking that tour brought their PT shorts. The charter buses were waiting for us on the dock. There were about 25 Marines and 25 Sailors on the bus. There was one Israeli bus driver and one Israeli tour guide who were very informative. When we arrived at the Jordan River, there were a lot of Israelis in the river. We changed over into our PT shorts and then walked out into the river. I waded out into waist-deep water, and it was just an amazing feeling that came over me – you knew and felt that it was holy. The background looked like a perfect picture. Many of the Israelis were older, and they were very friendly towards the Marines and Sailors. We were told by our Israeli tour guide that the Jordan River has healed Israelis with skin cancer and skin diseases. They would look at us, smile and wade through the water. Nobody bothered anyone. It was very peaceful. We also took the opportunity to swim in the Jordan River.

After we left the Jordan River, we went to Jerusalem. The tour guide showed us what is believed to be the area and route that Jesus walked as He was led to Calvary's tree to be crucified. This was awesome to be able to walk the same ground that Jesus once walked. Afterward we had some lunch, went shopping at the gift shops in Jerusalem, then boarded the bus and headed back to the USS Guam. We departed Haifa, Israel on 29 March 1991, en route to Rota, Spain. We arrived in Rota, Spain on 5 April 1991 for our final liberty, which was on base only.

On 7 April 1991, we departed Rota, Spain making our transit through the Atlantic Ocean and headed to the United States. During our transit back home, we didn't slack off. We still had Physical training and leadership training. Finally, we arrived at Morehead City, North Carolina on 18 April 1991. When the Marines offloaded from the USS Guam, there was the Marine Corp Band and a local high school band playing on the pier. As we came down the plank of the Guam with our sea bags, packs, rifles and gear, there were hundreds of Americans around the pier, along the coast and even in boats in the water, waving American flags and yellow ribbons, welcoming us home. You definitely felt proud to be a US Soldier. Some Marines kissed the ground when they were on the pier.

This one was over – we made it back not knowing if some of us would make it back when we departed for the war eight months ago from this very same pier. We did all that was asked of us, but the greatest accomplishment and reward was rescuing 281 civilians from over 30 different nations from war-torn East Africa in Mogadishu, Somalia who could have perished. We cannot forget those who made the ultimate sacrifice, who gave their lives for their country in Operation Desert Storm, and those that died from illnesses. Corporal Dennis Betz from our Weapons Platoon will always be remembered for his dedication, leadership and hard work. Their sacrifice will always be remembered.

We boarded the buses for our drive back to our home base, Camp Lejeune, North Carolina. As we were riding, all along the streets on both sides there were lines of people cheering and waving the American flag. When we stopped at one light, there was a married couple who wanted to get on our bus to give us two cases of beer (I was surprised our Platoon Commander let them). When we arrived in Jacksonville, North Carolina, the town right outside of Camp Lejeune, we received nothing but love from American citizens. When we reached the front gate of Camp Lejeune, there was a big banner hanging up that read "Welcome Home, Job Well Done". A few minutes later, the buses were pulling into the parking lot of 1st Battalion 2nd Marines, and anxiously waiting were wives, fiancés, girlfriends, sons, daughters, mothers, fathers, grandparents and friends. This was by far the best day for us in a long time. After all the hugs, kisses and reunions, we settled in and prepared for a well-deserved two-week leave period.

I was looking forward to going home to Indianapolis, Indiana to be with my family. I thank God that I made it back home safely without any serious injury. I recalled that as the 281 people we rescued from the US Embassy in Mogadishu, Somalia were preparing to offload from the USS Guam in Muscat, Oman, that many of them prayed silently that we would be spared the horrors of war, as with our help, they had escaped death and injury in the chaos of Mogadishu. Although we were trained and prepared to fight, we were spared the horrors of war just as they prayed. After the US Rescue Operation of the US Embassy in Mogadishu, conditions had continued to deteriorate in Somalia.

Two weeks after Operation Eastern Exit, Rebel Forces under Mohamed Farah Aidid drove President Siad Barre from Mogadishu and by May 1992, into exile in Kenya and Nigeria. President Siad Barre died in exile in Nigeria on 2 January 1995. Although many factors contributed to the defeat of Siad Barre and the collapse of his rule, Aidid was largely responsible for the final victory. He not only drove Siad Barre out of Somalia, but also defeated his three subsequent efforts to regain control. Mohamed Farah Aidid believed this success earned him the right to lead the nation, but other warlords disagreed. The clans could not unite to form a new government; warfare continued, and chaotic conditions persisted. In Mogadishu, the extreme violence made food distribution difficult, which made critical shortages in many parts of Somalia. Reports fostered an impression of widespread starvation, causing the United Nations to request international intervention to alleviate suffering and restore order. Opposition to the United Nations' intervention came from Mohamed Farah Aidid and his forces that controlled the Capitol Mogadishu. Aidid and his forces seized international food shipments at the ports. He used hunger as his weapon.

It was for these reasons that a year and a half after Operation Eastern Exit, US Naval Expeditionary Forces would return to Somalia once again "from the sea". Ten thousand US Marines from Navy Amphibious ships were sent into Somalia to provide humanitarian aid, break the military siege and restore order on a mission known as Operation Restore Hope. Food was delivered and order was restored. April 1993, Aidid waited for the Marines to withdraw and then declared war on UN peacekeeping forces based in Somalia.

In June 1993, Aidid's forces were responsible for ambushing and killing 24 UN Pakistani peacekeeping forces. In late August 1993, America's elite soldiers, US Army Rangers, Delta Force Operators, and the 160th

SOAR (Special Operations Aviation Regiment) were sent to Mogadishu to physically remove Aidid and restore order in the Capitol of Somalia. On 3 October 1993, US Delta Force operators and Army Rangers set out on a raid to capture several officials of Aidid's militia in an area of the Somali Capital City of Mogadishu, controlled by him. Although technically successful with the capture of several "tier-one personalities", the operation did not completely go as planned. Two US Army Blackhawk helicopters were shot down, and Delta Force operators and Army Rangers were trapped in the heart of Mogadishu, surrounded and outnumbered by thousands of armed militia. The brave US Delta Force operators and Army Rangers were engaged in a fierce battle with an overwhelming number of armed militia that lasted for hours. When the smoke cleared and as a result of the first battle of Mogadishu, between 500 and 1500 Somalis were killed. Also, 18 US soldiers and one Malaysian soldier were killed in action in the fierce battle, and one US helicopter pilot was captured.

The United States withdrew its forces soon afterwards, and the United Nations left Somalia in 1995. General Mohamed Farah Aidid then declared himself President of Somalia in June 1995, but his government was not internationally recognized. Indeed, within Somalia and even within Mogadishu, his control was fiercely fought over, especially by Ali Mahdi Muhammad. General Mohamed Farah Aidid died on 2 August 1996, as a result of gunshot wounds sustained a week earlier, possibly in a fight with competing factions.

It was very interesting to research the chain of events that triggered a reaction by US Military Forces, "Army, Marines, Navy and Air Force", in Mogadishu,

Somalia from January 1991 – the rescue of the besieged US Embassy to October 1993 – the first Battle of Mogadishu. I reflected back on having the opportunity to talk with some of the evacuees on board the USS Guam that were rescued from the besieged US Embassy in Mogadishu, 5-6 January 1991. As I listened to their account of those last horrifying days they spent in Mogadishu, not knowing if the US Rescue Force would arrive in time to save them, there was great joy in our hearts as both the rescuers and the rescued bonded, laughed and smiled together. It was rewarding to be part of a Rescue Mission that rescued innocent men, women and children that were trapped in the middle of a bloody civil war in East Africa. It is something we will always carry with us. After Desert Storm, I spent two more years at Camp Lejeune, North Carolina. I ended my stint in the Marine Corp at Marine Corp Base Quantico, Virginia where I was honorably discharged in September 1995.

I will forever cherish the memories I have from the Marine Corp. From the time I went to Boot Camp where young, raw teenage recruits were molded into Marines, to all the many adventurous journeys I experienced in the Corp. The Marines trained us to be mentally and physically tough. The Marine Corp taught us how to be strong leaders. We placed our boots on foreign soil to guard, to train, provide humanitarian relief, to restore order, to rescue innocent people and to fight in combat operations. When we were called, we would go where many would not want to go. But through it all, the greatest joy for me was serving alongside with my brothers. We were all one color, and that was Green. We partied together, trained together, lived in the same foxholes, and there were times when some Marines experienced their brothers dying in their arms in combat operations against enemy forces.

"We are a Band of Brothers." We are THE FEW, THE PROUD, THE MARINES.

Psalm 133 – "How good and pleasant it is when brother's dwell together in unity."

REFERENCES

AC-130H Spectre, AC-130U Spooky, Retrieved May 4, 2011 from
http://www.fas.org/programs/ssp/man/uswpns/air/attack/ac130.html

Bishop, James K., "Escape from Mogadishu," Foreign Service Journal (March 1991), p. 26-31.

Gellman, Barton (Staff Writer). Washington Post, "Amid Winds of War, Daring US Rescue Got Little Notice", pp. 2-3.

Mohamed Farah Aideed. Retrieved May 3, 2011 from
http://en.wikipedia.org/wiki/mohamed_farah_aideed

Ohls, Gary J... "Rescue... from the sea", pp. 127, 129-130, 133-141, 143-144.

Siegel, Adam, Eastern Exit: Evacuation Operation (NEO) from Mogadishu, Somalia in January
1991, pp. 7-8, 10-12, 14, 16-19, 22-25, 28-31, 33-39.

US Department of the Army: Analysis of Somalia, December 1993. Retrieved May 3, 2011 from
http://www.africa.upenn.edu/Hornet/horn_sml.html

Video Transcript, James K. Bishop – Mogadishu 1990. Retrieved May 3, 2011 from
http://www.usdiplomacy.org/accessibility/transcripts/bishop.html

Trent R. LaLand, is an Associate Minister at Emmanuel Missionary Baptist Church in Indianapolis, Indiana under the leadership of Dr. Darryl K. Webster, Senior Pastor. He is also one of several musicians in the Music Ministry and teaches teenagers in Sunday school. He has written a movie script from his book, "Night Mission to Mogadishu" in hopes of bringing this untold story to motion pictures. LaLand was one of the 60 heavily-armed Rescue Force members who were inserted into the US Embassy in Mogadishu, Somalia on 5 January 1991, on a daring and drastic Rescue Mission. He now resides in Westfield, Indiana.

TRENT LALAND

Visit **The Night Mission to Mogadishu** website at
http://www.nightmissiontomogadishu.com
Email: Trentlaland@mail.com

ORDER FORM

Order Form   (Print, fill out, mail with check)

Hayden Publishing 2400 Old Milton Parkway #202 Alpharetta, Georgia 30009

Title	QTY	Total	
			Total:

Book with a Signature (Add additional postage)	$3.95
US Postage (all items)	$5.95
CANADA (9% Tax)	$7.95
Tax	7%

Ship to Address:

Name:	
Street:	Apt/Box#
City: St: Zip:	

Checks or Money Order will be cashed and cleared before shipment. Orders can be placed online at Authors webpage.

Made in the USA
Columbia, SC
09 June 2021